Wait Forever

by Clare Lydon

First Edition January 2017
Published by Custard Books

ISBN: 978-1-912019-00-7

Cover Design: Kevin Pruitt
Editor: Laura Kingsley
Copy Editor: Gill Mullins
Typesetting: Adrian McLaughlin

Find out more at: www.clarelydon.co.uk
Follow me on Twitter: @clarelydon
Follow me on Instagram: @clarefic

Also by Clare Lydon

The All I Want Series

All I Want For Christmas (Book 1)

All I Want For Valentine's (Book 2)

All I Want For Spring (Book 3)

All I Want For Summer (Book 4)

All I Want For Autumn (Book 5)

Other Novels

A Taste Of Love

Before You Say I Do

Nothing To Lose: A Lesbian Romance

Once Upon A Princess

The Long Weekend

Twice In A Lifetime

You're My Kind

The London Romance Series

London Calling (Book 1)

This London Love (Book 2)

A Girl Called London (Book 3)

The London Of Us (Book 4)

London, Actually (Book 5)

Made In London (Book 6)

ACKNOWLEDGEMENTS

Wow, we're at the end of the journey with Tori & Holly, and I feel emotional but also happy to wish them bon voyage. They got their happy ever after in the end, and I hope you enjoyed the final book. It's a story that wouldn't be in your hands without the support and love of so many wonderful people — I don't do this on my own, every one of my books is a total team effort.

First up, thanks to Tammara Adams who is always a terrific and thorough first reader. She's closely followed by my early reading team who picked up errant typos and gave me general encouragement — you're all brilliant. A tip of the hat also to Lisa Jane, who answered my questions on living and working away from your partner with fantastic honesty.

As always, oodles of plaudits go to the fantastic quartet of my cover designer, Kevin Pruitt; my editor, Laura Kingsley; my copy editor, Gill Mullins and my typesetter Adrian McLaughlin. The four of you are worth your weight in fried gold. Plus, thanks to my gorgeous wife, Yvonne, for her constant encouragement and all the dinners she's cooked while I've been working away, getting this as polished as it can be. You're a star and I love you.

Finally, thanks to you for reading. 2016 was my first year as a full-time writer, and it was a successful year because of your support. Buying this book means I can write more, and your support means more to me than ever.

I really can't say it enough, but *thank you*.

Connect with me:
Tweet: @clarelydon
Instagram: @clarefic
Email: mail@clarelydon.co.uk
Sign up for my mailing list at: www.clarelydon.co.uk

To everyone who's followed Tori & Holly's journey.

This one's for you.

Chapter One

"To the left. Nope, a bit higher." Trudi took a step back. "Actually, could you move a bit to the right?"

"I'm on a ladder," Tori replied. "And my arm is about to drop off." Trudi was taking this far too seriously and it was Friday afternoon, nearly Friday evening. Surely they should be thinking about going home soon and slating the boss?

Only, Trudi was Tori's boss now, *and* they shared a flat, so that idea was a non-starter.

"What do you think? She's your girlfriend, after all." Trudi was referring to the enormous poster of Holly's face that Tori was currently holding a corner of. They were in a local bar, measuring up to hang the promo posters for Babe Magnet — and the promo posters were, basically, Holly.

"She looks gorgeous whichever way you hang it."

"You're a bit biased."

"Ask a silly question."

"You're right, though, she does look amazing — when's she coming over?"

"Four weeks and I can't wait." And Tori couldn't. They'd only been apart two weeks, but seeing as Holly had proposed the day before she left, it felt *way* longer. Tori already knew the next four weeks were only going to follow the same pattern: hollow days bereft of love, but filled with busyness.

"Go left."

"Seriously?"

"Yes," Trudi replied. "Up a bit." She clutched her chin as she peered up one of Holly's giant nasal cavities. "You know, your girlfriend has very smooth nostrils up close. Either that or the retoucher did a great job." She paused. "Stop. Put a mark on the wall just there — you still have the pencil?"

"I do."

"Then that's perfect."

Tori did as she was told, putting a faint pencil mark on the wall, before gingerly climbing down the ladder and rolling Holly up in a neat cylinder. Then she leaned against the polished wooden bar as Trudi hugged her.

"I've got a good feeling in my bones about this. We're going to put these launch posters of Holly up in bars all over the city, and then the Babe Magnet party is going to be the launch event to end them all."

"I agree. I've seen the drinks allowance."

Trudi nudged her. "It's not just that. This is all our hard work, everything we've been working towards over the past year, all presented to the world to use.

Babe Magnet is going to be the best lesbian dating app on the market."

"Don't forget the bisexuals, polysexuals, transsexuals, queers and undecideds."

"As if I would. We're inclusive, you know that." Trudi folded her arms as she shook her head. "Sometimes, I still pinch myself. We're in San Francisco and we're launching an app that Shauna and I thought up over breakfast last year."

"Was it a power breakfast?" Tori knew the answer, but she thought she'd play along for her friend.

"No, it was a bowl of porridge!" Trudi replied. "And now, here we are." She put an arm around Tori. "And I can't wait for your girlfriend to arrive either — she's going to be perfect as the face of Babe Magnet, and wait till the Americans hear her accent. They'll swoon all over again."

"She's from Watford."

"*I* know that, *you* know that, but the Americans will just see her face and hear her voice, then think she's been sent from heaven. You do know you're engaged to a superstar, don't you?"

A sizzling hot superstar, Tori thought, remembering the sex they'd had the night before she left: their first as an engaged couple. "I do now," she replied, her cheeks colouring as their intimate sex tape played in her mind.

Luckily, it was for her eyes only, and Tori was in no doubt she was exactly that: lucky.

Chapter Two

What had started out as a smattering of snowflakes had now turned into a full-blown snowstorm. Holly shook herself as she entered the bar, hoping to get rid of the excess ice that had attached itself to her in the short walk from the tube.

It was sod's law her first meeting since she'd been laid off was today, the day of snowmageddon, and *everybody* knew London went into meltdown in the face of even a centimetre of snow.

She did a quick scan of the hotel bar but couldn't see Ryan yet, so she claimed a sofa far away from the door and picked up the menu, scanning the overpriced items on it. When the waiter showed up, Holly ordered a coffee and a scone with jam.

She glanced out the window: the snow was still coming down in sheets. It looked pretty from the inside, but Holly knew the truth when it settled and turned into ice. Still, at least she was off her crutches now, with her leg on the mend. Crutches in this weather would not have been pretty.

A few minutes later she caught sight of Ryan dashing in through the main door, flicking snow from his shoulders as he scanned the room. When he saw her, he broke into a grin and did a little wave, before walking over.

Holly had always had a soft spot for Ryan: they'd been trainees together in the same recruitment company when they were fresh out of college, before Ryan left to join another firm.

"Great to see you!" Ryan gave her a hug, which she leaned back from to avoid getting too wet. Ryan's blonde hair was cut shorter than normal, but he still had the same gym-fit body as always. "You're still very tall, you know," he said, holding her at arm's length. "And still bloody gorgeous, obviously."

"And somehow, you still look like Brad Pitt in his prime."

Ryan gave her his widest smile that showcased his perfect teeth, a blur of polished white. With his boy-next-door good looks, Ryan was a favourite with men and women. He played on it no end, but at heart Ryan was a one-woman man, having married his childhood sweetheart, Eve, three years after graduation.

His wedding ring glinted under the hotel lights as he sat down, and Holly glanced down at her ring finger, still empty, even though she was now officially engaged.

She rubbed her finger as if twisting an imaginary ring and wondered what Tori was doing right now.

It would be just gone 10am in San Fran, so she was

probably drinking coffee with Trudi and working out how to snag more lesbians onto Babe Magnet.

With Tori in charge of the marketing effort, Holly had no doubt it would succeed. Her future wife was brilliant at anything she put her mind to, including loving her. Holly's stomach lurched at the thought: there was to be no loving her for the next four weeks — not in the flesh, at least.

"So how are things? If I know you, you're climbing the walls. Am I right?" Ryan ordered a beer from the waiter, and when he held up two fingers, Holly nodded.

"Weirdly, I'm not. I'm actually enjoying the time off — turns out after working full-on for the past five years, I needed a break and my body and mind are thanking me."

"I don't believe it," Ryan replied, putting a couple of beermats onto the glass-topped table in anticipation. "You're a workaholic. Or at least, I hope you are, otherwise this meeting might be a waste of time." He grinned as he spoke.

Her coffee and scone arrived and she set to work layering it up with cream and jam.

"I just ordered you a beer."

Holly nodded. "I know, but I ordered this first. Your company's paying, right?"

Ryan laughed. "Absolutely." He shook his head as Holly offered him half a scone. "Eve's cooking dinner, so no scone for me." He paused. "So I'll cut straight to the chase. I know you're not working at the moment, and right now we could really do with some help. So how are you fixed to come in and head up the contract side of the business for a few weeks? We'd make it worth your while, and you get to work with me again, which would surely be a dream come true."

Holly nodded, unable to reply as she had a mouthful of scone.

"It'll be like old times, except we get paid proper money," Ryan added. "What do you think?"

Holly swallowed, then cleared her throat. "When do you need me?"

"Is tomorrow too soon?"

Holly choked on her scone. "Yes — I have plans with my duvet."

Ryan gave her a grin. "Well, you tell me. We'd be lucky to have you, so whenever you can. So long as it's soon."

"Does Monday work?"

"It's going to have to, isn't it?"

Their beers arrived just as Holly popped the last of the scone into her mouth. She clinked her bottle to Ryan's when he held it up.

"Here's to the dream team getting back together."

"We worked together for six months, Ryan."

"But what golden months they were." He took a gulp of his beer before continuing. "So how are you coping without Tori? How long's she been gone?"

"Just over a fortnight — and it's weird. We're trying

to have daily chats, but the time difference is against us — when she's free, I'm asleep, and vice versa. But I'm sure we'll work it out. Right now, it feels like she's gone away for a few days and she'll be back soon." Only, Holly knew she wouldn't be: the only one waiting at home when she got back would be their cat, Valentine.

He nodded. "Eve went away for a month when she was training, and I hated it — we don't do well apart. I'd be a wreck if she was away for three months."

"Hopefully I'll cope — and I'm going to visit in a month. Plus, I'm the face of the brand, so she won't have to look far to catch a glimpse of what she's missing. I'm all over their marketing material."

"Really? How did you score that gig?"

Holly cocked her head: it was a question she'd asked herself. "I'm not exactly sure — I think I was conned into it one day when Tori's friend Trudi was over. Just because I'm over 6ft, people think I'm a model." She grinned. "I don't mind, though — I've got some fab photos of me for free, plus they're paying me *and* buying my plane ticket, so I can't complain."

Ryan grinned his boyish smile. "And it's a great way to keep you fresh in Tori's mind when all those US lesbians are flinging themselves at her. She just has to call up her app, and there you are."

Holly frowned at that. Would Tori have hordes of US lesbians knocking at her door? She hoped not.

"So how many weeks can you give us?"

"How many do you need?" She was still chewing over Ryan's words: she hated the uncertainty of being so far away. She trusted Tori completely; it was everyone else she was suspicious of.

"Probably four?"

"If the money's right, I can give you four."

"And it might extend, obviously," Ryan said, glancing out the window. "The snow's not letting up, you know. We might be stuck here all night. Shall I order another beer just in case they run out so we can toast the return of the dream team?"

Holly grinned. "Rude not to."

Chapter Three

Tori had been in the US for a couple of weeks, and she was acclimatising slowly. One thing she knew for sure was that *everything* was bigger: the fridges, the drinks, the roads, the cars, the opinions, the food. *Especially the food.*

Tori swore, if she carried on eating at the rate she was going, she was heading back to the UK around two stone heavier — or 28 pounds as the Americans would say. Yet all around her, all she saw were skinny Americans. It was a conundrum that didn't quite add up.

Even the bridges were bigger, like the Golden Gate. Tori had only seen it once after nearly two weeks of being here, because it had been shrouded in fog since the day she landed like some kind of mysterious artefact. The fog had cleared a couple of days ago, and ever since she'd skipped down to catch the landmark just in case it disappeared again.

Today, she was sitting on what she already considered to be 'her' bench, right near the Golden Gate, contemplating life without Holly.

Even though she was missing her, life in San Francisco wasn't all bad. First, she was in a new city, experiencing new things. Plus, she loved the service in America — everyone was so friendly *all* of the time.

She loved the drinks measures, too: they reminded her of mainland Europe. She recalled getting happily drunk on giant gins with Holly in Rome. That is, until Cara had nearly ruined everything by trying to snog her.

Bloody Cara.

The other thing Tori was a fan of was how everyone *loved* the way she talked. In London, her accent was nothing special, her pronunciation could even be accused of being lazy at times — her voice wasn't crisp and starched like Holly's. In contrast, in San Francisco she achieved the height of desirability just by opening her mouth and saying a few words.

However, there were obvious issues, too.

First, Holly wasn't here, and in Tori's downtime, she missed her like a physical ache. It was as if someone had chiselled out a piece of her heart and was holding it hostage.

She didn't *need* it to function, her blood still pumped and it wasn't necessary for her to enjoy her life; but she was always aware it wasn't there, always aware how much more balanced she'd be with it back in place.

Being away from Holly was making her lurch sideways.

She also missed her mum, which was odd, seeing as Tori only saw her every couple of months. But the distance between them was causing a sentimental reaction, and she'd almost cried on her first Skype call to her.

Finally, she missed her own space, which is why she was sitting on this bench. She missed coming home and being in her own flat — living with Holly didn't count, it had never been a chore. But now, as well as living in a new country, she was back sharing a flat with Trudi and Shauna. Friends who were a couple, friends she was living and working with 24/7.

Thank goodness they weren't the type to walk and find this bench. Right here, Tori felt like she'd found her own unique part of the city, something nobody else could claim.

When Holly arrived, she absolutely planned to bring her here and show her the bench she called home. It wasn't a patch on their bench in London, where Holly had proposed just a few weeks ago, but it would do.

Tori glanced down at her finger, and twisted her ring. She was engaged — she forgot that every now and again, it was still so new. When Holly finally got here, it'd feel like home, that small piece of her heart put back into place.

Chapter Four

Holly was sat at her hotdesk when it hit her: she really didn't want to work in recruitment anymore. She'd known that superficially when she'd left her last company, but she'd wondered if that was just because of the circumstances of her leaving, which had been less than stellar.

Recruitment was what she knew and was good at. If she didn't do it, what else was she going to do? That had been her thought process for the past week, as she'd sat in the flat with their cat, Valentine.

When Ryan had come through with the offer, it was an easy 'yes' to bring in some money and use the skills she had. However, working in this office with all these bright young things had only confirmed what she already knew: she couldn't come back to this, not full-time.

The accident had changed her. Getting run down on a zebra crossing and nearly dying had shifted her perspective on life, and now her heart just wasn't in the game. Like Take That had once sung, this was now someone else's dream — and that realisation made her breath catch.

She glanced to her left, where Ryan was sitting in his office, hemmed in by Perspex. He had a happy smile on his face and gave her a thumbs-up when he saw her looking.

She returned it.

Just this morning, she'd interviewed a new graduate for a position here. The woman had turned up in a pressed suit, clean shoes, her hair had sparkled and her skin had shone.

She'd fit right in, Holly had known it immediately, and she'd known within two minutes the job was hers. Ryan would love her, the clients would love her; she'd be successful at this and earn a lot of money.

She reminded Holly of herself six years ago: young, eager, fresh. But she wasn't that person anymore. Now, when Holly looked forward she didn't see herself heading up an agency as she had done even this time last year. Now, she wanted… well, if she knew that, she wouldn't be wondering.

She glanced at her watch: 4pm. She clicked on a wedding website she'd bookmarked, eyeing all the photos on show. Did she really want to walk down an aisle with rose petals on the floor and stand under a rose-covered arch? She was pretty sure the answer was no, and that Tori would say the same.

Holly's lips tweaked into a shy smile at the thought of Tori. It was 8am in America. She clicked on Tori's WhatsApp profile, but she hadn't been online since last night. She recalled Tori saying something about a breakfast meeting one day this week, but most of her time so far seemed to be spent in late-night meetings, usually in bars.

Holly shook her head and focused on the website, clicking on a link that took her to a wedding checklist. Flowers, photographer, cake, chair covers, music, table decorations. She filled her cheeks with air and blew out.

Wedding websites made her itch, especially ones covered in images of brides in flowing white gowns, the like of which she was never going to wear.

Maybe that should be her new career — a wedding website catering to lesbians.

It wasn't the worst idea in the world.

Chapter Five

"You might want to move the screen back a bit." Tori's head was enormous, taking up the whole screen. Holly loved seeing her girlfriend, but not up *that* close.

Tori did as she was told. "That better?"

"Much. So how are you?"

She looked tired, like she hadn't been sleeping or looking after herself. Tori didn't like to cook and she was working round the clock to make the app a success, which probably meant a diet of coffee and snacks, which was clearly playing havoc with her complexion.

Despite that, though, Holly still wanted to reach through the screen and kiss her. However she looked, Tori was always beautiful to her.

"I'm knackered. We were out till 3am at one of the big club nights, and then we have a 10am meeting this morning to discuss the launch, which is getting closer every day and we still don't have enough staff. Trudi is in a right tizz and Shauna's working round the clock on the code. It's manic."

"They're making you earn your money, then."

Tori adjusted her screen again. "I don't know what I was thinking giving up my cushy desk job."

"Don't forget abandoning your fiancée."

"How could I?" Tori gave Holly a tired smile. "At least I didn't drink as I was on duty, so I'm just tired." She scratched the side of her face. "And how's our little boy doing?"

Valentine was sat on Holly's lap, pawing the screen. "He's saying hello."

"I can see." Tori paused. "Hello Valentine!" she said, her pitch higher than normal. "Do you miss mummy?"

Valentine meowed in response.

"I miss you, if that helps," Holly said.

"It does, and I miss you, too." Tori pouted. "How's being back in an office?"

"It's making me see recruitment is not for me — not unless I want my soul to shrivel up and die."

Tori screwed up her face in a frown. "I'd say no to that option."

"Me, too. So plan B it is."

"Which is?"

"To be confirmed." She paused. "However, I am going to see that venue with my mum at the weekend, so I can let you know on that. Looks gorgeous."

"The one I sent you? The manor house? The one with the moat and the bridge? The one straight from a film set?"

"The one where royalty could well have got married. Yep, that one."

Tori clapped her hands, then followed it up with a pout. "I'm torn — I'm excited about you going, but I want to go with you."

"I know," Holly said. Doing this with the help of her mum was fine, but it wasn't the same as planning it with Tori. This was meant to be an exciting time for both of them, yet right now, she felt sad and alone.

"Being here sucks when we're trying to plan a wedding."

"And going to these venues with my mum sucks."

Tori pursed her lips. "So life's pretty sucky."

"It is."

"I bet your mum's thrilled you asked her, though."

"She's tickled pink." Holly paused. "But I'd rather go with Sarah."

"Imagine if your mum found out you'd rather go with your step-mum. *Ouch*."

"I know." Holly paused.

She could see Tori, she could imagine how she smelt, but she was still *so* far away. "It's not the same talking through a screen, is it?"

Tori gave her a sad smile. "It's as good as we can do right now."

"I mean, I can see your breasts, but I can't *touch* them."

"I might have known you'd bring it back to breasts," she said with a grin.

"It's your fault for having such fantastic ones. I miss them and I miss *stupid things*." Holly paused. "Like you leaving your clothes all round the flat; you missing the shelf with your keys most nights and the clatter as they fall on the floor; and your baffled face as you try to work out what to do with microwave rice." She gave Tori a sad smile. "I miss all of it."

"I know what to do with microwave rice!" Tori sounded indignant.

"You do — burn it."

"It happened once."

"And how many times have you cooked it?"

Tori grinned. "That's not the point," she replied, sighing. "And I miss you, too — mainly going to sleep with you and waking up with you. And you cooking me dinner — it feels like I'm back at university, living with Trudi and eating cereal for dinner, along with the occasional pizza."

"Try not to get scurvy before I arrive, okay?" Holly said, laughing.

"I'll try," Tori agreed. "It's not long till you're here, and when you are, I promise I'll let you cook me dinner, and that my breasts will be extra-attentive to your needs."

"They will?"

"Uh-huh."

"Smart breasts."

Tori gave her a grin. "Babe, I have to go, sorry — it's coming up for 10am and I have this meeting." She checked her watch, then looked off to the side. "Shall we do the same time at the weekend? I have so much to do before then."

"And maybe a little FaceTime sex then, too?" Holly said. Tori had promised her nakedness for the past week, but her schedule had been too busy. Holly had been working out all sorts of moves and angles in her absence.

Tori grinned. "Sorry, I'm distracted." She wiggled her mouth, before settling on what Holly guessed was meant to be a sexy pout. "I won't be distracted at the weekend," she said, in her best femme fatale voice.

"Better," Holly replied. "I climbed our hill the other day, sat on our bench, but it was just weird. I got all sad thinking about how happy we were last time we were there."

"Stop being so maudlin — take Ryan to the pub, he'll take your mind off it."

"Actually I have a date with Kerry coming up, it'll be nice to see her." Kerry was an old friend of Holly's from university, who'd just been travelling the world and was back in London briefly. "She's planning on coming to the US."

"Really? Have you told her I'm in San Francisco? That should stop her coming to California." Tori made a face at the screen like she'd just eaten something bad.

"Good to see your opinion of Kerry hasn't changed."

"Well, has she changed?" Tori raised an eyebrow at the screen.

"She's been travelling round Asia for the past two

years. She might have gone Zen and read up on all sorts of stuff, like how to behave when your old mate's girlfriend is around. She might surprise you."

Tori snorted. "Kerry won't change, she likes the way she is. Combative I believe is the word. And she didn't think much of me when I was just your friend, so I'm sure she was thrilled when she heard we were getting married."

"She said congratulations, actually."

"I'll reserve judgement."

"Well, I'll report back when I've met her. I said she could stay for a bit till she flies to America, so she's taking the spare room."

Tori nodded. "Makes sense," she said. "Just don't leave her alone with Valentine. She might corrupt him."

Tori grinned at her own joke and Holly rolled her eyes.

"So we're agreed on an October wedding date — you'll see what they have available?" Tori added.

"Yup — leave it with me." Holly paused. "Have a great day, babe."

"You too, love you."

"Love you, too."

There was a noise as the call disconnected, and then the screen just showed an image of Tori from around three years earlier. Holly stared at it for a few moments before shutting down her laptop and leaving the meeting room.

As usual, after speaking to Tori, Holly was on a temporary high. However, she knew that in a while she'd come crashing down, as if she'd just eaten a block of Cadbury's Dairy Milk and necked a vat of coffee.

When she got back to her desk, Ryan was still in his office and beckoned her in. She stuck her head into his space.

"Fancy a drink? Eve's out for the night with work, which means I've got a free pass."

Holly slumped against the doorframe, weighing up her options. Valentine might frown at her, but a drink was just what the doctor ordered.

She gave him a nod. "We can't let a free pass go to waste, now can we?"

Chapter Six

The following evening, Sarah paid Holly a visit on her way home from work. Since the accident, Sarah had slipped seamlessly into being one of Holly's close friends, which was weird seeing as she was married to her dad.

"How are you coping on your own?" Sarah asked, shrugging off her coat and sitting down on Holly's L-shaped couch. Outside the window, the trains rattled by, their window ledges thick with a January frost.

"I'm okay — and it's only a few weeks till I fly over. I'm doing a bit of recruitment work with an old colleague, too, so that's keeping me busy." Holly handed Sarah a glass of Merlot, before sitting down next to her with a glass of her own.

"Not falling back into it, I hope?"

"Nope, just a few weeks and I couldn't turn down the cash. Doing it freelance alongside something else could be the way to go, to keep the money coming in."

"Look at you getting all entrepreneurial," Sarah replied. "And how are the wedding plans?"

"Mum and I are going to see a venue Tori and I both

love, so I have high hopes." She clicked her fingers together. "And by the way, did I ask if Elsie could be flower girl?"

Sarah smiled. "You did not, but if you offer her a lovely dress and the chance to show off, I'm sure she'll be all over it."

Holly laughed. "I'll stop by at the weekend to ask her."

"And you know, if you need any help with the wedding — anything at all — just ask. I remember planning ours and help was a lifesaver."

"Thanks, I might take you up on that," Holly replied, sipping her wine. "So how was your day?"

Sarah sighed before replying. "Let's just say I'm happy to be having a drink. It was just one of those days when everyone I work with drives me insane. A bit like you working in recruitment, I do sometimes wonder how I fell into the insurance business, you know?"

Holly nodded — she knew *exactly*.

"But after last year, with my tumour and everything, I'm beginning to see things differently: blurred, but different." Sarah laughed at her own joke. "It was after something you said — about me being a good listener."

"You're the best listener I know."

"Thank you," Sarah replied. "And I was wondering if maybe I could do something with that? Change career, maybe become a counsellor. Maybe for people who've suffered brain tumours or life-changing injuries. When you've been through something like that — as I know you understand — having someone who really gets it is key.

"And after today, I know that stressed execs worrying over ridiculous stuff isn't important. However, helping someone sort their head out after they've nearly died is." She paused and took a sip of her drink. "Alcohol is also important, by the way," Sarah added.

Holly laughed and took a slug of her wine — she loved the way it slipped slowly down her insides, warming her as it went. And she totally agreed with Sarah: things that used to be important to her just weren't anymore, but helping people recover *so was*.

"Weirdly, I was considering doing something similar — something to do with injuries. I'm not sure I'd make a great counsellor, but maybe I could do physio? I read up enough about it when I was recovering from my accident." The thought had skated through her mind before, but it was the first time she'd said it out loud, even to herself.

Sarah nodded. "Why not? Right now, you probably know more about it than many so-called experts — and you can talk to people in *real* language. Most of the staff I dealt with were brilliant, but some needed better people skills, and that's putting it gently."

Holly nodded. "My rehab people are great, they've really inspired me. I've been thinking about them a lot in my time off — that maybe I could volunteer at the centre a day a week to get the feel of it. What do you think?"

"Sounds great — I'm really proud of you."

Holly blushed. "You don't have to be proud of me — you're not my parent and I'm not eight."

Sarah laughed and brushed Holly's arm. "I can be proud of you just the same. Look at where you were a few months ago. I remember sitting with you in the park — you didn't know what you were going to do with your life, and your leg was a metal detector's dream."

"It still is a bit," Holly replied, touching it gently. Her leg was *so* much better now, but she was always aware of it and its potential for pain.

"Now you can walk, you've left your job and you're talking about retraining. This is big news and you should give yourself a pat on the back. Your dad will be proud when I tell him, too."

Holly tilted her head. "Can you not tell him just yet? I mean, I'm only saying all this out loud for the first time today, so I need time to think it through, look into options. I haven't even told Tori yet."

Sarah nodded. "Of course — I won't say a word."

"Great," Holly replied, appeased. "And how is dad doing? Still going bald?"

Sarah's face lit up at the mention of him; a similar face to the one Holly pulled when someone mentioned Tori.

"He's doing great. Work is good and he's chilled out a bit now I had a scan and it came back clear — did I tell you that?"

Holly shook her head. "You didn't, but that's terrific."

"It is," Sarah said, nodding. "I tell you one thing, though — through my whole brain tumour and recovery, Elsie's been the one who's really made the difference, giving us something to focus on. Without her, I think David might have fallen apart, but he didn't. She's at nursery now and loving it — before you know it, she'll be a teenager."

"A teenager? Stop, you're making me feel old." Holly took another sip of her drink. "Have you looked into any courses yet?"

Sarah nodded. "Yup — a few today when I was tearing my hair out."

"Maybe we could set up a practice together in the future, who knows? You do the mind, I'll do the body. Holistic recovery. We've even got the same surname."

"Just so long as people don't think I'm your mother," Sarah said, with a shudder.

"Or my lover."

Sarah threw back her head, laughing. "Oh god, I hadn't thought of that!"

Holly grinned. "Don't worry — we'll put a sign over the door that says 'Wicked Stepmother & Step-Daughter'. Sound good?"

"Sounds perfect," Sarah said.

Chapter Seven

Tori wasn't wearing the right bra — this one was too tight. She'd meant to change it before she left and now she was sitting at her desk, wriggling her torso and trying to snag one of her fingers under the band. It had been annoying her all day, and she didn't see that changing anytime soon, especially because they were going straight to a bar to meet some press and bloggers later. She wriggled a bit more, but it was a lost cause: she was just going to have to suck it up.

The build-up to the Babe Magnet launch party was going at some pace. Today was the first time they were showing off the app to a bunch of journalists — and Tori was in charge. But she was confident it would go well: charming people was her bag. Plus, between her, Trudi and Shauna, they knew the app back to front. Trudi and Shauna especially, seeing as they'd created it.

"Ready for today?" Trudi was sat at her desk, typing and talking at the same time. This had been Trudi's default position since they'd landed in America: Shauna assured Tori this was normal, that this had been their life since they'd conceived Babe Magnet almost a year ago.

"Born ready, you know that."

"And that's why I hired you," Trudi replied, flashing Tori a wide smile. "And you're looking very gorgeous, by the way, which is never a bad thing."

"Did you just hire me for my looks?" Tori rolled her eyes.

"No, but the fact you're cute doesn't hurt."

"No selling me off to the highest bidder later, okay? I'm the marketing director, nothing more. Plus, Holly would be really pissed."

Trudi clutched her chest in mock horror. "Would I do that to one of my best friends who's also working really hard to make our business work?"

"If it meant Babe Magnet would get more coverage, I'm inclined to say yes," Tori said, laughing.

"You have a very low opinion of me."

"I've known you a very long time."

"Besides, I'm your boss, not your pimp."

"Isn't that one and the same?" Tori asked with a grin.

* * *

Seeing as their office was a tiny hovel downtown, they'd decided to decamp to the far more chic Mission district for today's press meet-and-greet.

The bar Tori had chosen was called SideCar. An intimate setting, it had acres of scuffed wooden tables and chairs, low lighting, an impressive horseshoe bar and a gargantuan burger menu — 25 to choose from. That was another thing Tori had noticed about the USA: they liked their burgers. London's burger selection had grown considerably in the past couple of years, but it had nothing on America.

The manager of the bar was Dominic, a friendly guy with more hair on his chin than on his head. And as with all US bar staff, he couldn't do enough for you, including offering them copious cups of coffee and soda. Tori turned down his third offer, lest she need the loo mid-presentation.

The Babe Magnet banners were up, the demo phones and tablets had been tested… now they just needed an audience.

"What time are they due?" Tori flicked her hair off her forehead — she needed a cut, but choosing the right hairdresser in a new city was almost as daunting as being thrust out into the dating scene again. She needed an app for hairdressers.

"About five minutes," Trudi said, looking up from her laptop. "And will you relax? You're making me nervous."

"You're making me nervous, too." Shauna had her Dodgers cap on backwards, as she'd favoured ever since moving to the States.

"But *aren't you nervous*? I mean, this is different to all the other times I've done this for clients," Tori said. "Then, they'd hired me and I was representing them, it wasn't a matter of make or break — but this *is*. If we don't get coverage, people won't know we're here. And we've all uprooted our lives to do this — I've left my fiancée and it's your *baby*, for fuck's sake. Aren't you even a little bit nervous?"

Tori rubbed her hands together and bounced on the balls of her feet. She was wearing her green Converse, her lucky ones.

"I wasn't before you started saying all of that, but I am now," Trudi replied, her face now markedly paler than it was before.

At that moment, a woman walked into the bar, stopped to ask the barman something, and he pointed towards Tori: it seemed their first journalist had arrived.

Tori straightened her shoulders and fixed her face with her best smile, holding out a hand, which the woman took.

When she did, Tori recoiled. "My god, your hands are freezing." And then she mentally slapped herself. That wasn't the first thing she'd intended to come out of her mouth in their first press meet.

The woman, though, seemed to take it in her stride. "Blame my mother, cold hands are hereditary in my family," she said, with a laugh. "I'm Melissa, from The Chronicle."

Melissa's dark hair was short and stylishly cut — maybe Tori should ask for her hairdresser's number? She was around the same height, too, with a relaxed air about her, and her short fingernails were painted a hot shade of pink.

"Great to meet you. I'm Tori, and these are the creators of Babe Magnet — Trudi and Shauna."

Melissa shook both their hands, accepted a glass of wine from Dominic and sat at the bar.

"So, British accents — is that an act to impress us, or is it for real?"

In contrast, Melissa's accent was deliriously Californian, dripping with laid-back cool.

"All for real," Tori replied. "Although we're hoping to improve our Californian accents while we're here."

"Are you living here?"

"Yup — we've moved from London."

Melissa nodded, looking impressed. "Big move," she said, hanging her bag on the hook under the bar, before retrieving her tablet.

"It was, but we're loving it so far. Especially bottomless Sunday brunch — that's to die for."

"It is — I can tell you some great places to go to if you like, seeing as you're all the new girls in town."

"That would be great," Tori said, smiling.

"But a word of advice," Melissa said, pointing a finger at Shauna's head. "Lose the Dodgers cap."

Shauna removed it right away, running a hand through her long, dark hair. "Really?"

Melissa nodded. "Really. An LA cap in a Giants town? If you want to make friends and influence people, lose it.

Or better yet, buy a Giants cap. I know you're British, but others might not be so kind."

"She's not even a Dodgers fan, she just likes the colours," Trudi added.

Melissa laughed. "Then buy a Giants cap. But definitely don't wear that," she said, pointing at the offending headwear. "And don't worry, your hair still looks fine."

Shauna gave her a grin. "I'm just going to the bathroom to check — thanks for the tip."

Tori watched Shauna go before turning back to their guest.

"I'm really looking forward to hearing all about your app." Melissa flashed Tori a warm smile, before firing up her tablet.

"And we're looking forward to showing you — we're hoping it's going to revolutionise the lives of women around the globe. Are you single?"

When she asked, Melissa turned her gaze on her, a corner of her mouth turning upwards, along with the corresponding eyebrow.

Tori slapped herself mentally again: she hadn't meant it like *that*.

"I am," Melissa replied. "So maybe it can help me." She paused, assessing Tori. "Are you?"

Tori shook her head abruptly, holding up her ring finger. She didn't want any misunderstandings about this — she'd had enough of those since she and Holly had hooked up to last a lifetime. "Very unsingle in fact," she said. "Newly engaged."

Melissa avoided Tori's eyes now, but nodded her head. "Well, congratulations."

"Thanks," Tori said. Melissa was the first stranger she'd told, and she had to admit, it felt kinda awesome.

* * *

Three hours later, Tori, Melissa, Trudi & Shauna were sitting with fresh cocktails, along with three other journalists who showed no sign of wanting to leave.

The presentation had gone well, but Tori knew this was the part that mattered: getting to know them over a few drinks, while trying to stay somewhat sober throughout.

She was doing that, but Trudi seemed to have got a little excited at her own free bar, currently flailing her arms in conversation with a journalist called Kevin. At least Shauna was holding down the fort with the other two and didn't look quite as excitable.

"We used to have an LGBT section in the paper — but then, like all the lesbian bars, it disappeared. Now, it's just seen as mainstream news, but staffing levels are at an all-time low, so you really have to fight to cover stuff like this. But I happen to think this is going to be huge, so I was able to convince my boss." Melissa smiled at Tori. "Plus, I get to come and hang out with British girls and listen to their accents all night. It's a win for me."

"And a win for us," Tori replied. She wasn't joking, either. All the journalists had been positive about the design and usability of the app, but Tori had got along particularly well with Melissa: they'd just clicked from the off.

"It's too bad your girlfriend isn't here, though — you must really miss her, being so far away." Melissa held Tori's gaze as she spoke.

Tori nodded: that was the understatement of the year. "I do, but she's flying over in a few weeks. I can't wait to show her around, she's going to love it."

Melissa fished in her bag and handed her card to Tori. "Before I forget," she said.

Tori glanced at the card, before putting it in her back pocket.

"I'll drop you an email with brunch places and good restaurants to go to — I'm friends with the food and drink editor, so I know what I'm talking about.

"In fact, I get offers of free food and drink all the time, so I'll drop you a line if I ever need a plus one." She laid a hand on Tori's arm. "And that wasn't a come-on, honest," she continued, with a pained smile. "It's just that I like to have a list of friends to take to these things and I just thought, you're new in town, you'd appreciate it more."

"I really would, you've no idea," Tori said. "Plus it'd be ace going out with someone in the know."

"I won't steer you wrong, I promise," Melissa replied with a grin. She checked her phone, then frowned, before putting it back in her bag. "I have to run — got a story to type up before tomorrow."

Melissa hopped off her chair and grabbed her coat and bag, before holding out a hand to Tori. "It was really lovely meeting you, and I'll do everything I can to help you get this app off the ground."

Those were exactly the words Tori was hoping she'd say. "Thanks so much — see you around sometime soon for brunch or drinks."

"Count on it." Melissa squeezed Tori's arm, before saying her goodbyes to the others and giving Tori a final wave.

Tori watched her go, before picking up her drink and moving up the table to join the rest of the group.

She had a good feeling about Melissa: she was going to be useful professionally and she might even become a friend. And having a real American friend would be the first step to Tori settling into her temporary home.

Chapter Eight

"Can you see me? You keep going a bit fuzzy." Holly tilted her head one way as if that might help. It didn't.

"I can see you fine, but the sound keeps going in and out. It did this last time. Have you tried walking around the room with it? What about going more towards the train tracks?"

"It's colder by the window."

"It's never cold in that flat."

"It is right now, believe me. It's minus three outside and Valentine has even stopped jumping on the window ledge — I think it's too cold for his paws."

Holly stared out the window into the evening gloom: London was currently covered in a thick snow duvet. Soon, nothing would be running and the apocalypse would be declared. At least she had a good stock of Hob Nobs in the cupboard to keep her going.

"Poor baby," Tori replied. "Hang on, I think that's working okay. So what's going on with you? You said you had big news?"

"I do," Holly said, steadying the tablet on her lap. "Are you sitting down?"

"I am now."

"Well." She paused. "I'm going to retrain as a physiotherapist, working with people who've had accidents."

Tori looked suitably stunned. "Wow," she said, eventually, her face not giving much away.

"Well say something else other than wow. What do you think? Good idea? Crazy idea? I talked it over with Sarah, and she thinks it's a go — she's thinking of becoming a trauma counsellor herself."

"I can see Sarah doing that, she's got that aura about her."

Holly frowned and her stomach flip-flopped, for all the wrong reasons. "But not me?"

Tori shook her head. "I didn't mean that. I just mean, Sarah seems wise, whereas… shit, this isn't coming out very well is it?"

"You could say that."

"What I mean is, it's a bit more leftfield for you, but it's good. It's just a big jump from city recruiter to physiotherapist, you have to admit."

Uncertainty licked Holly's face like an excitable puppy — this was still a new idea to her, so she had hoped she was going to get Tori's support on this.

"That's kind of the point. I mean, I was getting disillusioned with my job, and here's something I'm passionate about, where I can make a difference to people's lives. I know what they're going through because I've been there myself — *am still* going through it myself." As if on cue, her left leg gave a twinge of pain. "Just think of the empathy I can bring."

Tori was trying to rearrange her face into a positive formation, but it was taking longer than Holly would have liked. Eventually, she adopted a semi-smile, and nodded slowly. "I get it, I really do — and I think you'd be great."

"It'd be a massive pay cut, obviously, but it feels like the right thing to do. Plus, I can still freelance at recruitment while I'm training to pull some money in."

"I haven't seen you this excited about something since Southampton nearly got to the FA Cup final, so I say go for it. If it's what's in your heart, babe, then it's right."

Holly's heartbeat sped up. She missed Tori calling her babe — her life was empty without it. "I think so, too. I've already looked into courses, and I could start in September in the new academic year."

"Blimey, you don't mess around."

"Nope, I'm all fired up." Holly paused: she hoped Tori was truly behind this idea and not just paying her lip service, because this was something that was going to affect the rest of their lives. "But you really think this is a good plan?"

Tori nodded, going a little out of focus as she did. "In a way, this kinda makes sense. You love learning new things, and if you put your mind to this, you'll be great. Plus, you're a good listener, so you'll be able to help them in a holistic way, rather than just fixing their aches."

Holly sat back, weighing up what Tori had just said. "So you think I'll be okay at it?"

"I think you'll be brilliant."

"Good. Because I'm pretty set on the idea already." She paused. "And how about you — are you looking forward to me landing in two weeks' time and sweeping you off your feet?"

Tori grinned into the camera, so wide it almost took up the whole screen. "Can't wait," she said. "And I've made a list of everything we have to do — good job you're here for ten days as there's a lot to fit in."

"And how's the job going?"

"Loads to do, not enough time. We took some journalists out for drinks the other night and gave them a demo, and there was lots of interest."

"As there should be."

"And Trudi booked the photographer for you the other day, too, to add to the shots you already did in London. Those look *amazing*, by the way."

"They're pretty good, aren't they?"

"Beyond that. Anyway, the new ones are booked to happen on the day you get here, so be sure to look pretty from the plane. Not that you wouldn't." Tori paused, giving a huge sigh. "I can't wait to see you. I sound like such a sad sap, don't I?"

Holly smiled, shaking her head. She knew exactly what Tori meant. "If you do, then I do, too, but it's not long now. It's very odd to get engaged to someone and then for her to disappear the very next day."

"I know — I don't feel like we had a chance to celebrate. Not properly."

"We'll do it in San Francisco — drinks, dinner, sex hanging from a chandelier, the works."

"Sounds perfect," Tori replied, grinning. "I'm counting down the days."

Chapter Nine

Three days later and Tori was walking along the Bay on a Friday afternoon, getting some fresh air and grabbing a late lunch. The pavements were thick with tourists and the air hung with the smell of sugar from the surrounding stalls, along with the diesel from the tour boats going out to Alcatraz.

To her right was a beer pub — or bar as the Americans would say — selling over 100 different types: it looked very tempting after the day she'd had.

Tori was working with an agency to place a bunch of ads across all the key social media outlets, and she was having an issue with the woman doing the graphics. The woman seemed set on doing what *she* wanted to do and not what Tori, the client, had asked.

Tori had wanted to go to Trudi to complain, but Trudi and Shauna were working flat out just like her, and she didn't want to bother them. This was her brief, her department, so she'd just have to manage it.

It was at times like this she missed her old boss Sal to talk things through with and bounce ideas off.

Having worked with her for the past few years, getting in sync with Trudi and Shauna was proving harder than she thought.

When she got back to the office, she got a text from Melissa: would she like to meet for a drink after work tonight? Tori stared at her phone. Maybe she would. Tonight was one of the first evenings she'd had off, and it might be nice to get together with a local and see some other sights.

She texted her straight back, and Melissa duly texted the name of the bar. Tori set about her afternoon's tasks with a little more gusto, knowing that tonight she could relax. She grinned at Trudi over her laptop, only her friend had a strange look on her face, staring intently at the screen.

"You okay?" Tori asked.

Trudi snapped out of her stupor quickly and nodded her head. "Sure." She moved to cover the screen, then stood up and grabbed Tori's hand, pulling her into their lone meeting room.

"Now you're acting really weird." Trudi's grip was no-nonsense, and Tori pulled her arm away, rubbing her wrist as she did.

"Sit, please," Trudi said, holding out an arm.

"What's going on?" Tori didn't like the tone Trudi was using one bit — she'd heard it before in their long history as friends, and it was never good news.

"So there was a journalist there the other night — Kevin. You remember him?"

Tori nodded, recalling the red-headed guy with the cute smile. "I do," she said. "You were chatting with him a lot."

"We were. In fact, we stayed on, had a few more wines after you left. And he caught me later on, when my mouth *might* have been a little looser than normal."

Tori's stomach lurched: 'looser than normal'. What did that mean, exactly? Because Tori knew from experience that when Trudi got a little drunk, little white lies dropped from her mouth like fairy dust.

"What did you do?" Tori asked. "Is this like the time at university when you told everyone I was related to the King of Norway?"

"A little, yes," Trudi said, running a hand through her flowing hair, her face running through a gamut of expressions, all of them laced with regret. "But the long and short of it is I *might* have led him to believe that you and Holly met on our app, and he's using that story in his write-up."

"What? But we didn't meet on Babe Magnet — we've known each other for nearly 20 years!" Tori didn't know what to think. "What on earth made you say that?"

Trudi's face contorted into a semblance of contrition, but not enough to convince Tori it was real.

"Look, I was just a bit drunk, he'd heard you just got engaged and he was asking me about the success of the app beta phase. It just… slipped out. I mean, it's a *tiny* white lie to *one* website, but I just thought I'd give you a heads-up."

Trudi knotted her hands together in front of Tori, her face creased with concern. "And yes, I know I shouldn't have said anything like that, but I don't know, it just… happened." She paused, looking Tori in the eye. "Can you forgive me? Let Holly know? I mean, like I said, it's only a small website so it's not like it's a major issue."

"But it is up on the web, correct?"

Trudi nodded. "Uh-huh."

"The web that's available all around the world?"

"Technically, yes — but what are the chances that anyone in the UK will read a gay site in San Fran? Minimal, I'd say."

"Until it's picked up by a bigger site and goes national."

Trudi clasped Tori's shoulders with her hands. "I'm sure it won't come to that," she said. "And if it does, it's great publicity for the site and I promise I'll make it up to you — you know how you met." She paused. "It was a momentary lapse of judgement, and if you want to blame anyone, blame Dominic from the bar who just kept topping up my glass."

Tori shook her head at her friend. No, it wasn't the end of the world, but she'd prefer Trudi's drunken motor-mouth to be a thing of the past and not infiltrating into their present.

"Let me call Holly and let her know, just in case she sees it," Tori replied. "I'll let you off this once, but try to keep a lid on your gob from now on — perhaps lay off drinking so much booze at your own events?"

Trudi nodded, her eyes wide. "Absolutely, I totally agree. And Shauna's already told me off, just FYI."

Tori frowned. "As she should."

Trudi held up three fingers. "I promise, guide's honour, that no other lies shall pass these lips. Only gorgeous words about you and Holly. And you're welcome to use the Babe Magnet Uber account to get her from the airport when she arrives."

Tori stood up, straightening out her shirt and trousers as she did. "You're going to have to do better than that, but that's a good start," she replied. "How about getting me a coffee for starters?"

"Coffee with a dash of milk, coming right up," Trudi replied, rubbing her hands together.

***

The bar Melissa had chosen wasn't far from their apartment, which Tori was glad about. After Trudi's little gem of news, she needed somewhere away from them tonight, albeit somewhere she could easily stumble home from.

She ordered a lemon drop, then sat down in one of the scratched wooden chairs, still thrilled at the sea of American accents she was floating in. She'd always been impressed with a US accent — she blamed Netflix.

While she waited for her guest to turn up, she tortured herself by pressing the button on her phone, flicking to the site that had run the story. Three hours later and she could already see it was getting shared a whole lot on social media, which she should be thrilled about — this was great PR for Babe Magnet, after all.

The story showed an image of her from the Babe Magnet press kit she'd prepared — at least it was a flattering image — replete with a screenshot of her Babe Magnet profile, which she'd agreed to mock up to showcase the app.

So now, at a casual glance it looked like she was on Babe Magnet, looking for love; and if you read the article, you'd believe Babe Magnet had *found* her love.

Tori exhaled, drumming her fingers on the table: working and living together with her friends was proving problematic. She was *totally* invested in Babe Magnet, not just because of Trudi but also because she thought it was a brilliant product. She just wished Trudi would make it easier to get behind her, too.

Melissa bounced in a few minutes later, giving her a wide smile when she saw her. She grabbed a cocktail — apparently all drinks were called cocktails in America, even a vodka and tonic — something Tori was learning.

"Great to see you," Melissa said, arranging herself in her chair. "And you got a seat — good work."

"I try my best."

"And I see you're famous after the other night, too. Good image of you." Melissa flashed her phone at Tori, and an image of Tori stared back. "You never told me you and Holly met on Babe Magnet."

"That's because we didn't — Trudi made it up when she was drunk the other night."

"Ah," Melissa said, clenching her jaw. "And how do you feel about that?"

Tori shrugged. "Like Trudi said, it's a little white lie and it's getting us publicity, so it's not the end of the world. But then again, it's not *true*," Tori said. "But apparently, we're living in a post-truth world now, and fake news is all the rage."

"Unfortunately that's very true," Melissa replied, laughing gently. "What does Holly think?"

Tori pursed her lips: it was at times like these she hated the distance between them — she didn't need any unnecessary misunderstandings between them when they were on opposite sides of the world.

"I left her a message," Tori replied with a sigh. "Best I could do at 4am UK time."

"I forgot the time difference. You might want to, though, because it's being shared — you've got 22 retweets so far."

"Really? Is it a slow gay news day today?"

Tori's stomach sank. She'd done nothing wrong, so why did she feel guilty about this, like she was being unfaithful to Holly even by having a Babe Magnet profile in the first place? Trudi had promised her it'd go no further than their offices, yet here it was, on the front page of this website. She'd told Tori she'd give them *her* profile for the story, not Tori's.

Bloody Trudi.

But Melissa was unperturbed. "I wouldn't worry about it. I'm sure your girlfriend will understand, and if nothing else, you look really cute in that photo — it's a good shot."

"Thanks, I think," Tori said, sighing. "But I'd still rather there wasn't an article floating around the world showing everyone my Babe Magnet profile and lying about my life."

"I bet Trudi and Shauna are loving it though, am I right?"

"They wouldn't be that gleeful to my face, but they were looking very happy when I left them alone tonight."

"I think you might have to chalk this one up to experience. This is the first article out and it's doing well. Back it up with mine at the weekend and the others that'll come out soon, and you could have a hit on your hands."

"You might be right. This is just one of those moments in life where you have to let the universe take you where it wants to, right?"

"No-one said it was easy," Melissa replied. "You're in show business now."

Chapter Ten

Holly met her mum at the art deco mansion in south London just before midday. It was a brisk January Saturday, but the snow had cleared and the sun was shining weakly — it was easy to imagine what it would look like on a brighter, warmer day. Its website had shown an incredible house with period architecture at every turn, and the real-life exhibit was no less impressive.

It even had a bridge over a pond in the garden, and a sweeping lawn perfect for those shots that every bride craves, apparently.

"This looks very grand — are you sure we can afford this?" Holly's mum was wearing her best coat and Holly would bet she had on her best clothes underneath, too. For her mum, coming to something like this was like going on a date. She'd already told Holly off for turning up in jeans.

"That's what we're here to find out, although the rates on the website didn't look too scary — not compared to some places. We saw one place online where they wanted five grand just to rent it, no food and drink included."

Her mum's mouth dropped. "No food included? I'm glad you didn't take me there." She paused, walking up the mansion's wide drive. "In my day, we had a church and a church hall — there wasn't a choice. And in a way, maybe that was a good thing."

Holly smiled: she was glad her mum was comparing their wedding to her own. "Maybe so. But a church wouldn't take Tori and me."

Her mum reached over and squeezed her hand. "You know what I mean."

And she did. Holly took a deep breath, smiling at her mum.

This was it: the first place she was going to look at for her wedding.

Her and Tori's wedding. And honestly, she'd never thought she'd be able to get married in her lifetime.

But times had changed, society had changed, and Holly was thrilled this was now an option — but most of all, she was thrilled to be marrying Tori.

Holly grinned as she conjured an image of Tori in her mind, lying in bed with a post-orgasmic smile on her face.

"What are you smiling at?" her mum asked, nudging her daughter with her elbow.

Holly shook her head, a blush creeping onto her cheek as her feet crunched on top of the gravel drive. "Nothing."

She cleared her throat before tugging open the thick wooden door. The smell of must and damp hit her as she entered the main hall. It was wood-panelled and high-ceilinged, shaped like a hexagon with doors leading from every side.

Holly wrinkled her nose as they approached the front desk, where a woman with thin-framed glasses and wavy brown hair was writing something down. She looked up, giving them a pinched smile and a not-too-subtle once over.

"Good afternoon," the woman said, her smile not widening. "Is one of you Holly?"

"That's me," Holly said, holding out a hand.

The woman shook it limply. "I'm Fiona," she said. "Would you like to follow me?"

Fiona led them through to a main hall off the grand foyer, glinting in the lunchtime sunshine that was flooding through the windows. The walls were adorned with period paintings, and round tables were already set so you could visualise your big day.

And to Holly, it all looked mightily depressing. Chair covers were wrapped with peach bows, table centrepieces glinted under the lights, and the uber-floral carpet made her head spin.

Her step-mother Sarah should be here: floral was her thing, she'd love it.

"So this is the main room where you'd get married, and also where you'd have your wedding breakfast and then your evening reception," Fiona said, giving them a weak smile again. "You'd have the room from 9am on the day you're married and our curfew is midnight. You get to choose from three menus and you can come in for a tasting session, too." She paused. "The groom couldn't make it today?" She fixed Holly with her half-smile again.

She really needed to work on that.

Holly smiled. "Actually, it's another bride — I'm marrying a woman."

Fiona blinked, then recalibrated herself ever so slightly. "Righteo!" she said, her voice a little too high-pitched. "Lovely, of course, so sorry, I didn't have it down in my notes. So it's bride and bride, that's… terrific."

Fiona didn't know where to look, her gaze bouncing all around the room — anywhere but Holly. "We don't get many l… " she said, then paused, not wanting to say the word.

"Lesbians?" Holly offered, almost shouting the word to see Fiona's reaction.

She wobbled, like Holly had just thrown the word at her like a giant rock. "Right, l… not many ladies, what with the prices being what they are. I read somewhere that same-sex couples usually have to foot their own wedding when families don't approve, but I can see that's not the case here." She grinned towards Holly's mum, almost begging to be rescued.

"No, there's none of that here," her mum said, her tone shrill. "Myself and Holly's dad couldn't be happier with her choice of partner, and we're all looking forward to the big day, aren't we?"

"We certainly are," Holly said, feeling distinctly uncomfortable under Fiona's intense glare.

Perhaps this place wasn't going to be their perfect venue, after all.

Fiona nodded, her face stuck in half-smile mode. "My cousin is a… gay," she added. "Single though, so not getting married anytime soon." Fiona paused, and the silence that followed took up the whole room. "She's been through a lot of girlfriends though," she added. "It seems to be the way, doesn't it?"

Holly cringed outwardly and inwardly. She looked at her mum, whose face spelt alarm, too. She was willing Fiona to stop speaking anytime soon, but she wasn't sure she was about to. She'd dug her hole and she seemed keen to keep going.

"But it's great you've found someone and you've decided to marry them." Fiona rubbed her hands together awkwardly. "We haven't had any gay weddings here yet, so this would be a first."

"You surprise me," Holly replied,

"It's not that we haven't had couples in, it's just they never seem to come back." Fiona looked at them, baffled.

Neither Holly or her mum said a word as the air in the room soured.

"Anyway, would you like to come through to the conservatory and we can get some hot drinks and talk through the packages we do?"

Holly's mum nodded. "That would be lovely. Lead the way."

Holly gave her mum a large eye roll as they walked out of the room.

In her pocket, her phone vibrated: Holly pulled it out. It was another missed call from Tori; she'd put her phone on silent for the viewing, and she could see she had two messages now, too — her reception had been buggered earlier. Why was Tori so keen to get hold of her?

She'd find out when she was done with Fiona.

Chapter Eleven

"And then she proceeded to just keep calling Tori the groom, then keep correcting herself. And she asked if we'd still want the bridal suite that night — where does she think we might like to sleep?!" Holly took a breath. "It was kinda funny in a way, but really, Fiona needs to work on her soft skills."

"I want to meet Fiona. Maybe you should invite her to the wedding. She sounds like a closet case to me." Kerry was sitting in The Arches with Holly, a beer on the table in front of her, shaking her head.

"If she is, she should stay in there."

"So it's a no-go?"

"I think so — even mum was in agreement. It was a lovely building, lovely setting, but I don't know, I just didn't like the vibe. Fiona didn't help, but I just couldn't see us getting married there."

"Back to the drawing board, then."

"Yep. I'll do some looking around, see where else I can find." Holly paused. "So how is it being back after how many years?"

Kerry yawned, stretching her long arms over her head. With her tan and her dark hair shaped into a sharp bob, she looked radiant, like living abroad suited her.

"Two," she replied. "And it's weird. Nothing's really changed that much, but I have. I've got itchy feet already, and I've only been back three days. You're a life-saver letting me stay."

Holly shrugged: she had the room, so it made sense for Kerry to move in. "Not a problem."

"I'll pack up and bring my stuff over in the morning?"

"Sounds fine — it'll be nice having the company."

"Now that Tori's buggered off you mean? That's got to hurt — you ask her to marry you and she leaves the country?"

Holly gave her a look: she'd been waiting for Kerry to have a dig. Only, now Tori was her fiancée, things had changed. Kerry was attacking her love, rather than her friend — and the difference was huge.

"It was planned, you know that." Holly paused. "And lay off Tori, she's my future wife now. Plus, aren't we all older and wiser? Can't we all play nicely now?"

"Where's the fun in that? Me and Tori have a love-hate relationship and I've always enjoyed it."

"She sends her love, by the way," Holly said, even though she'd done no such thing. Where Tori was concerned, her feelings towards Kerry was mutual. They tolerated each other, nothing more.

"You're such a liar," Kerry replied, laughing.

"So how long are you staying in London? I'm sure we need nurses here, too."

"Yes, but the weather's not so good, is it?" Kerry said. "Although if I meet the love of my life in the next couple of weeks, then it might be forever." Kerry paused, stroking her chin. "But if that doesn't quite work out, then two or three weeks. I need to work out my new itinerary and also see where the work is." She paused.

"San Francisco was on my list actually, and if you're going to be there, maybe I'll hit that up first. If Tori's starting this new dating app out there, maybe it can work for me."

Kerry shifted in her chair. "Talking of which, have you seen you're being mentioned when it comes to Babe Magnet? Apparently, you found love there, too."

"Apparently," Holly said, discontent rumbling through her. She'd missed chatting to Tori about it as yet, but she'd listened to her voicemail and got the gist, so she knew it was Trudi's doing and out of Tori's control.

Holly wasn't surprised, but it didn't stop her being a little riled at Trudi getting some mileage from her life and her relationship.

Holly could just imagine Trudi telling Tori it was all part of her marketing role, to big up the brand. Tori had already intimated that Trudi's new-found status as tech entrepreneur had gone straight to her head.

"I guess I'll have to let it slide and be the supportive fiancée about it, because I can't really kick off when they're just about to launch the app. But from what Tori's told me, this is pure Trudi. She's got a one-track mind and she'll say anything if it makes the story easier to sell."

"At least she didn't make Tori un-engage you — be thankful for that."

Holly rolled her eyes. "I suppose I should be." She paused. "But seriously, first Trudi makes us go camping at Brighton Pride, which I still haven't forgiven her for. And now she's saying we met on her app when we met at school *years* ago — that's stretching the limits." She gave Kerry a resigned smile. "But what can you do?"

Holly leaned over and grabbed the phone from Kerry's hand, reading the first paragraph of the article for a second time, as well as casting her eye over Tori's profile again.

"At least it's a good photo of Tori, so she'll be happy." Holly knew if there was to be a silver lining from this, that was it.

"Even if it is her profile on a dating website," Kerry replied.

"You're meant to be making me feel better," Holly said, giving Kerry a look.

"What? I said she looked hot." Kerry gave her a grin. "Come on, it's kinda funny, saying you met on a dating website when you've known each other so long."

"Maybe I'll see the funny side in the morning," Holly said, shaking her head. "Tori and me are solid, I'm not worried about that." She paused, running a finger down her bottle of pale ale.

"Honestly, I'm more worried she's not coming home when her three months are up."

The temperature in Holly's blood sank lower as she contemplated the silent fear she was only now articulating. She hadn't meant to bring it up — heck, she hadn't even processed her own thoughts properly — but there it was, out on the table, flashing like a neon light.

"I mean, she loves me, she wants to marry me, I'm pretty sure of those two things. But this app has come at a really bad time, what with planning a wedding and all."

"Can't you postpone the wedding till she's back? You haven't found anywhere yet — aren't you just putting pressure on yourself where you don't need it?"

Holly sighed: it'd flitted through her mind they could do that, but then again, they'd both been adamant they didn't want a long engagement. They'd waited so long to get to this point in their lives, both of them just wanted to tie the knot this year, no later.

"Maybe, but neither of us want a long engagement. That was quite important when we talked about it."

"But couldn't you put it back three months, maybe even six? That's not that much longer, and it'd take the heat off you?" Kerry took a sip of her drink as she held Holly with her gaze.

"Kinda feels like giving up if we do that, though, like giving in. I don't want to wait, but I also don't want Tori to still be living in America when we get married. We got engaged and she flew the next day. I don't want the same thing to happen in our marriage — I want to be together."

"And you should be," Kerry said. "But you know what, you should be having this conversation with Tori, not me."

Holly nodded, a weight settling over her heart. She knew that, but what with them being so far apart and Tori so busy, it wasn't as easy as it sounded.

"You guys can make this work, I believe in you," Kerry added, putting a hand on Holly's arm. "And if you need help, I can be your wedding slave for the next couple of weeks. Once I get my next job sorted out, I'm yours to use."

"Really?" Holly said, a smile tweaking the edges of her mouth. "That's the best news I've had this year. Everyone says they're happy to help, but they've all got their own lives. I thought I'd have more time, but now I'm working full-time and trying to plot my next course of action, it hasn't worked out that way."

Kerry stood up. "Think of me as your white knight on a shining horse, trotting in to the rescue. I can help with arrangements, but you have to sort your relationship. Deal?"

Holly nodded. "Deal," she replied.

***

When Holly got home that night, she slammed the front door, then wished she hadn't as Valentine jumped and ran away. She followed him into the lounge and flicked on the light, sitting down on the sofa and sighing.

Her initial brush-off of the article was wearing thin when she looked at her phone and saw she had three texts from friends saying they'd seen Tori's Babe Magnet profile in the article and was everything okay?

She texted them back to say everything was fine — why did everyone always assume the worst? Was it a British thing?

Ever since Tori had left straight after their engagement, Holly had sensed the unspoken judgment in people's reactions. And while, yes, she knew how it might look, if her friends really knew them, they'd know Tori taking a job overseas was just bad timing. Or perhaps their engagement had been bad timing? Whatever, having Tori's dating profile splashed across the front of a lesbian website wasn't helping much.

She also had a text from Tori: 'Sorry babe, been trying to call you. Call me when you get this. x'

She sighed and threw her phone onto the sofa, happy as Valentine reappeared and jumped on her lap. He was just what she needed.

"Hey there little buddy," Holly said, stroking his ginger fur. "What's your other mummy doing over there in San Francisco? Do we need to call her to find out?"

Valentine ground his paws into Holly's thigh in response as he circled her lap, getting comfortable.

Holly winced as his claws snagged her leg, before

putting a call into Tori's mobile: it rang three times before a strange voice picked it up.

"Hello?"

"Tori?" Holly asked, even though she knew it wasn't her voice. She checked the screen to make sure she'd dialled the right number. Yes, she had. She put the phone back to her ear.

"Nope, it's Shauna," said the voice. "Who's this?"

"It's Tori's long-lost fiancée."

"Holly! Great to hear from you." Shauna's voice was far jollier than normal.

"Is Tori there?"

"You've just missed her: she's gone to collect some marketing stuff with Trudi — she'll be back soon. You want to call back in a bit?"

"It's gone midnight here."

"Right." Shauna cleared her throat. "Have you seen the article? Great picture of Tori."

A hot flash of annoyance rumbled through Holly. Of course she'd seen it, she wasn't living on the moon.

"I have — apparently I should be thanking you for bringing us together." Holly tried to sound cross, but she could never be too cross with Shauna — she'd always liked her, and she loved how she put Trudi in her place when she needed it. Shauna was the right partner for Trudi, and Holly had seen quite a few wrong ones.

"I'm sorry about that — just Trudi and her big drunk mouth shooting off, you know what she's like."

Holly nodded, even though Shauna couldn't see her. "I do," she replied. "I just wanted to hear Tori's voice, I suppose."

And it was only when she said that out loud she realised *why* she'd rung. Tonight's conversation with Kerry had stirred up a melting pot of emotions, and Holly's foothold in the world was a little less sure than it had been this morning.

"Of course," Shauna said. "She shouldn't be too long."

Holly sighed. "That's okay — just let her know I called, will you? I'll speak to her tomorrow when I wake up."

"Okay," Shauna said. "And Holly?"

"Yep?"

"She's really missing you, too, if that helps."

Holly smiled at that. "Strangely, it does," she replied. There was a pause and Holly heard some noise in the background. "Is she back?"

"She is, hang on," Shauna replied.

There was a pause and then Tori's voice on the line. "Hey babe, so glad I caught you."

"Me, too." Holly's face flushed red, but she felt calmer already. This was all it took.

"You're up late."

"I've been texting people telling them we're fine after they saw your dating profile online."

"Do people have nothing better to do?" Tori asked. "They know I'm working for Babe Magnet, for god's sake. And if you want to blame anyone, blame Trudi —

but she's promised to treat you like royalty when you're over, and she has serious cash to spend."

Holly heard somebody shouting in the background.

"Trudi says hi and that she loves you," Tori said, laughing gently. "I'll tell her you'll love her back eventually, shall I?"

"Tell her she's not making my life any easier — first she steals you away, now people are worrying about us." Holly paused. "But there's nothing to worry about, is there?" She was pretty sure there wasn't, but she needed reassurance tonight.

But from the sound of Tori's voice, which softened immeasurably when she spoke, she understood. "Nothing at all — and the article clearly states we're engaged," she said. "Stuff like this always feels worse when we're apart, but it's nothing, really. Just my dating profile online and a tiny white lie." She raised her voice. "And Trudi's buying us a massive wedding present to make up for it, aren't you, Trudi?"

Holly heard a noise in the background and grinned — she could just imagine Trudi's tongue stud banging against her teeth as she nodded. She smiled, despite herself.

"I think I just needed to hear your voice," she said. "I'll leave you alone now, I'm off to bed."

Tori paused. "Wish I could come keep you company."

Holly smiled, her mouth squeaking as she did. "I do too, more than you can possibly imagine."

Chapter Twelve

When Holly got home from work the following Tuesday, she walked in to find Kerry sitting on the sofa, Kindle in hand, with Valentine sprawled by her side purring contentedly.

"Are you trying to steal my cat's heart? Isn't there an unwritten lesbian rule that says you can't do that? It's nearly as bad as stealing my girlfriend, isn't it?" Holly was standing with her hand on her hip, scowling at her cat's traitorous behaviour.

"I can't help it if your cat is a born flirt."

"You're not wrong," Holly replied, walking round the sofa before collapsing next to Kerry. When her weight hit the cushions, Valentine opened his eyes and gave her a look of distain.

"You're in the bad books," Kerry said, putting down her Kindle.

"All that time spent bonding with him, and he just casts me aside." Holly wrinkled her nose as she drew in a big breath. "Something smells good."

"There's a fish pie in the oven — my mum's special recipe."

"You're going to make someone a delicious housewife one day."

"I know," Kerry said. "Beneath this gruff exterior is a heart of gold and the cooking skills of Nigella. If only they could see it."

"Perhaps you should put it on your Babe Magnet profile."

"You might be right."

"Of course I am — the way to a woman's stomach is through her heart."

Kerry cocked her head. "Isn't that the other way around?"

Holly grinned. "You might be right — the other way makes you sound like you want to dismember them."

"You're not going anywhere near my profile," Kerry replied, before slapping Holly's thigh. "Cup of tea for the hard worker?" she asked, getting up.

"I'd prefer a beer," Holly said.

"Coming right up."

* * *

Holly was enjoying having Kerry around: she was happy to cook most nights, which was a real bonus. On top of that, when it came to their wedding, Kerry was revealing herself to be a hopeless romantic. All of which meant she was throwing herself into the wedding search with gusto, which Holly could have kissed her for.

Getting someone on board to help was just what she

needed, but it also highlighted that this wasn't exactly how she'd wanted her wedding planning to go. It should be her and Tori doing it together, not Kerry doing it on their behalf. Still, she was a willing and able helper, so Holly wasn't going to look a gift horse in the mouth.

When Holly got home last night, Kerry had four venues shortlisted, she'd found a pop-up gin bar to hire, a caterer and decorations galore. And while Holly didn't think the inflatable zoo was quite what they were after, the rest of her options were inspired.

Holly wasted no time in booking appointments to view all of Kerry's venues, including a mill house she loved the look of and knew Tori would, too. What's more, Sarah had volunteered to drive them, which was perfect.

Now she just had to keep her fingers crossed that one of the venues came through, *and* that it was available when they wanted it.

She'd texted Tori earlier to tell her Kerry had found them the perfect venue, and waited for the response. It had duly arrived in five minutes.

'Kerry has found us the perfect venue? Kerry who is living with you Kerry?'

'The very same.'

'Who knew she had her uses?'

'She cooked me a delicious fish pie last night, too.'

'Wonders will never cease.' And a minute later: 'No running off with Kerry.'

'No flaunting your Babe Magnet profile.'

'Touché.'

'Besides, Kerry's more likely to run off with Valentine.'

'No letting Kerry steal our pussy!'

'No letting Kerry near any pussies in this house — is that what I'm hearing?'

'That pretty much covers it,' Tori had replied.

Chapter Thirteen

Sarah picked Holly and Kerry up on Saturday morning in her blue Beetle, and they made their way to south London to begin their mammoth day of wedding venue viewing.

First up had been a hotel, which they'd all turned down on behalf of its lurid carpet which looked like it hadn't been changed or cleaned since the 1980s: "Nobody wants to get married standing on that," Sarah had rightly stated.

Then they'd seen a pub with a fantastic main room big enough for their proposed 80 guests, but they'd been put right off by the toilets, bright pink and with questionable flooring. Third, they'd viewed a palace on the outskirts of London, but that had been way over budget, and frankly, nothing Holly aspired to.

It was now 4pm and Holly's features were slumped into a frown. Sarah was trying to cheer her up by drip-feeding her Werther's Originals toffees, and the trio were putting all their chips on the mill house in east London coming up trumps. They'd all loved it online, but online and in the flesh could often be a very different vibe as today was proving.

Holly rolled her eyes as the sat nav informed Sarah she'd gone down the wrong street. "I don't think that's your fault — isn't that what your sat nav's for?"

"You'd think. But every time it sends me the wrong way, it blames me. A bit like your dad. In fact, I've nicknamed the sat nav Dave 2."

Holly and Kerry both laughed at that, brightening the despondent mood in the car.

"Whoever knew that wedding venue shopping could be this bad?" Kerry said, leaning forward in between the two front seats like a five-year-old.

"I did," Sarah said, putting up her left hand. "I've done it recently enough and the scars are still there. For something that's meant to be such a joyous day, it's always stressful and expensive." She paused, glancing at Holly. "But it's only as stressful as you make it, always remember that. When we scaled ours back, it felt so much better and we had a perfect day."

Holly sunk down a little in her seat, guilt flushing through her. Sarah might have had the perfect day, but she had certainly not been the perfect guest. "You did," she said. "Shame you had a grouchy step-daughter in tow for it."

Sarah smiled. "I knew you'd come round eventually. Well, I hoped you would, and I was proved right, wasn't I?" She gave Holly a smile. "And anyway, I've got a feeling in my bones about this one: the grounds, the stream, the lovely fairy lights they had in that picture-perfect courtyard? Even if it's only 75 per cent as lovely as it was in the pictures, it's still going to beat what we've seen so far, isn't it?"

Holly nodded. "Very true," she said through a mouthful of toffee. And then Sarah turned a corner and the mill house came into view, and Holly got pinpricks all over her body.

She'd never had those before. Well, not over buildings, anyway.

That was a good sign, right?

"Oh my god, it looks better than it did on the website — how cute is it?" Kerry was leaning forward again as Sarah swung the car into the drive.

Ahead of them was the old stone mill house, now restored beyond its former glory, gleaming like a jewel in the January sunshine.

They parked the car and got out, admiring the grounds, the crisply cut lawns and the just-so flowerbeds. First impressions count, and this looked perfect.

"You know what I most liked about this one?" Holly said, as she let her gaze take in the understated grandeur of the venue. "It wasn't just a parade of men and women getting married on their website. They'd thought about it, and there were pictures of two women and two men, too. It really makes a difference."

"I thought that, too," Kerry said. "Let's hope the inside and the staff don't let it down, shall we?"

"Fingers crossed," Sarah said as she followed Holly through the wooden front door and into an incredible, high-ceilinged room, with perfect arched windows and buttery sunlight streaming in. The remarkable feature at one end of the room was an old water-wheel, standing around 15ft tall, encased in glistening glass.

Holly stood stock still, goosebumps breaking out all over her body. "This could be the place. I have to video this for Tori." She got out her iPad. "In fact, bugger that, I'm going to call her now."

Holly hit the green button on FaceTime and waited for Tori to pick up — which she did after four rings. She looked sleepy, which she was, seeing as her head was still on the pillow.

"Hey gorgeous — you awake?"

"Not really," Tori said, rubbing her eye with the heel of her hand. "Where are you?"

"We're at the mill house — just about to do the tour and I thought you might want to see it, too."

Hearing that, Tori opened both eyes wider and sat up with a struggle, smoothing out her hair. "Okay, I'm awake now," she said. "Just don't show me off too much."

Sarah stuck her head over Holly's shoulder. "We've got a crack team here to give the on-the-ground verdict — me, Kerry and Holly."

Kerry stuck her head over Holly's other shoulder. "Hi Tori! Whoa, you look a little different to your Babe Magnet profile picture."

Tori gave a smile that was 100 per cent fake. "Ha ha," she replied, narrowing her eyes before rearranging herself in her bed. "So let's see this place, then — I've seen you lot a million times before."

Just at that moment, a man approached in a suit, looking official. He was well groomed and his teeth were ultra-white — Holly's gaydar rang immediately.

"Holly?" he asked, the epitome of bright and breezy, his white collar starched, his striped tie offering a hint of jaunty.

"That's me," Holly said, holding out a hand.

"Miles," the man replied. "Lovely to meet you. I know you said your fiancée couldn't join you, so I'm assuming these two ladies are just friends?"

Holly turned the screen to Miles. "This is my very sleepy partner, currently in San Francisco and just woken up. Say hello to Miles, Tori."

Tori looked startled, but styled it out. "Hi, Miles!"

Miles grinned at the iPad. "Come with us, Tori. You're going to love this place, and then we'll book you a wedding you'll never forget."

Tori sat up that little bit straighter in her bed. "I'm all yours, Miles," she replied.

"Lead the way," Holly added, excitement flowing through her veins. She glanced down at the screen as they started to walk towards the water-wheel. "I'm so pleased you're here, too. This feels right."

Tori nodded. "It does. Like we're doing this together."

"And wait till you see what's ahead. The water-wheel is incredible."

"You look gorgeous," Tori said, grinning.

Kerry jumped back in. "No sappiness — today's about business."

"Bugger off, Kerry," Tori said.

And then Holly spun the iPad round, so Tori could get a look at the water-wheel.

They all heard her gasp out loud. "Oh, wow!"

They might just have found their venue.

Chapter Fourteen

"I tell you, that one night with that lot of press has netted us a ton of publicity," Trudi said, holding up her coffee cup to Tori. "You're a genius for arranging it."

"Not really a genius, but I'll take it if that's what you're offering," Tori replied, smiling.

They were sitting in the coffee shop in the bottom of their building, and Trudi had been so enthused, she'd been waving her hands around like she'd just learned a dance routine and was keen to practise. Thankfully, she now had a sandwich to keep her hands busy.

The shop was packed, with all of its ten tables taken up with hungry Friday workers. Tori wasn't surprised: its house sandwiches and salads were so flavourful, they almost made her weep.

She was having the Mexican chicken chipotle flatbread, which was all sorts of awesome; while Trudi was currently chomping on a salmon, watercress and horseradish on brown. The smile on her face said it all. When she'd swallowed, she put down her sandwich and began her hand-dancing again.

"And did Shauna tell you the regret being poured out all over Twitter and Instagram over the fact you're engaged?"

"She might have mentioned it," Tori said, her face pained. Working with Trudi should come with a health warning.

"You're a hit in San Fran, girl!"

"Terrific, just what I wanted to hear. I'm engaged, remember?"

"You people who want to tie yourselves down with patriarchal notions and labels."

"I thought we agreed to disagree on our views on marriage?" Tori scowled at Trudi. "And aren't you meant to be being nice to me?"

Trudi held up her hands. "It was a joke! You know I'd never do it, but I'm all for you getting hitched. I understand equality just as much as the next woman."

"Glad to hear it."

"But honestly? You flashing your Babe Magnet profile and your British accent, and then telling everyone you're engaged? A million lesbian hearts broken," she said, snapping her fingers together. "Just like that — I heard them cracking right down the middle. It's like when that one from One Direction announced his engagement."

"Which one?"

"I don't know — the one who left?"

"He didn't stay engaged."

Trudi rolled her eyes. "That wasn't my point," she said, rubbing her hands together. "But you know what? This is seriously all coming together so well. And when Holly gets here, you'll be less mopey and it'll be brilliant."

Tori scowled. "I have not been mopey."

"Much," Trudi scoffed, before holding up her hands. "But you're allowed, don't get me wrong — I don't know how I'd cope if I had to be away from Shauna for all this time."

Tori had her ideas, but she kept them to herself. Trudi always seemed delighted when she was out on her own, free to roam as per her and Shauna's agreement to have an open relationship. But still, they were each other's primary partners, so she guessed it would still be hard.

"Plus, I wanted to let you know — the Babe Magnet launch party is going to double up as your engagement party. It's the least we can do after claiming we got you together." Trudi had an Olympic-sized smile on her face, looking very pleased with herself. "What do you think?"

Tori sighed, shaking her head. "That you're using our relationship as a marketing ploy again?"

Trudi drew back, a hand on her chest, her face showing mock horror. "You try to do something special for your best friend, and this is the thanks you get," she said. "I'd really like it if you accepted. I'm even going to throw in a fancy dinner wherever you like while Holly's here. Just to show you I am sorry." She paused, looking Tori in the eye. "What do you say?"

Tori gave a rueful smile. What could she say, apart from yes? "That would be lovely, thanks," she said, as Trudi leaned forward and hugged her.

"It's going to be great, you just wait," Trudi whispered in her ear.

"But no reiterating the fact we met on Babe Magnet because it's not true," Tori said, pulling back, searching Trudi's eyes. She wasn't sure if she spotted sincerity in them or not.

"Cross my heart and hope to die," Trudi replied.

Chapter Fifteen

The day had finally arrived: she was picking Holly up at the airport, and her body ached with the anticipation of seeing her partner. Outside, the sky was grey, but inside, she was sunshine and butterflies all the way.

Tori glanced around the airport, taking in its glass roof, neat splurge of shops and shiny white floors. It was so clinical, it almost seemed of another time, somewhat space age.

Only six weeks ago, all these signs and shops had been alien to her, but not anymore. She was a different person now, with different ideals and a whole new life. But while she might be living in the US, the missing piece of her heart was on its way from the UK, safely stowed in Holly's luggage.

When the board said the flight had landed, Tori deposited her coffee cup and walked to arrivals, not wanting to miss the moment when Holly appeared. Her blood was pounding in her ears, her face flushed with excitement. Nerves and adrenaline rushed around her body as she readied herself to see Holly again: she was like a kid at Christmas.

Or rather, she was like herself *every year* at Christmas.

And then, 20 minutes later, Holly appeared: that was one advantage of having a tall girlfriend, she was always easy to spot.

Holly scoured the crowds, searching her out; Tori put up her hand, waving. She wished she'd brought a red rose, but she hadn't been able to find a florist in the airport. How did everyone else do those romantic reunions she saw on TV? They were clearly far better organised.

When Holly finally spotted her an infectious smile slid across her features, and she almost sprinted to the end of the line and swooped down, picking Tori up off her feet. If Tori had secretly longed for a Hollywood reunion, she was getting her wish.

Holly spun her around and the rest of the airport tuned out as Tori soaked up Holly's embrace, clinging to its warmth and swagger. Holly gripped her tightly, her hands secured around her back as she spun Tori around once, then twice, her emotions in a similar whirl. The roughness of her coat grazed Tori's cheek, but she didn't mind.

Damn, she'd missed this woman. And now, with her head resting on her fiancée's shoulder, inhaling her familiar smell, Tori relaxed for the first time in six weeks; whatever worries she'd been carrying with her when she woke up this morning simply evaporated into thin air.

Eventually, Holly put her down, her lips landing on Tori's ear, her cheek, then finally, her lips.

And when they did, Tori's spirit and heart soared, their kiss causing sparks to rain down her body, lighting it up for the whole airport to see. Tori reached out and gripped Holly's arms as she wobbled with emotion, sinking into their silver screen kiss.

This kiss was just the two of them, back where they belonged, getting the reunion they deserved, lifted by love.

It was a while before they came up for air, and then they simply stood, arms around each other, grinning.

"That was some hello," Tori said, reaching up and kissing Holly again. "Have you missed me?" Even though she knew the answer, she still needed to hear it from Holly's mouth.

"More than I ever thought possible," Holly replied, her eyes smiling down at her lover. "I still can't quite believe you're in front of me. It seems like a dream."

"I know," Tori said. "I was nervous to see you, can you believe that? I mean, *it's you*."

Holly nodded. "I can believe it, because I felt the same. I started getting jumpy on the plane, wondering how it was going to go." She paused, touching Tori's face. "Everyone's warned me that it might take time to get used to each other again, but I'm only here ten days. So you think we can speed up the process and slot back into each other right away?"

Tori raised an eyebrow at that. “I’m sure it can be arranged.”

“Good,” Holly said, kissing her again.

She began to walk, taking Holly’s hand: it fitted perfectly, just like always. Tori glanced shyly up at Holly, who was watching her intently.

“So we’ve got a chauffeur-driven car, all paid for by the company. I hope you’re impressed.”

“It’s the least Trudi owes me, which I’ll tell her when I see her. I thought she promised me flowers as well?”

“Maybe she’ll bring them to the photoshoot.”

“Maybe.” Holly held up Tori’s left hand which she was holding, and smiled. “Just checking you’ve still got your ring on. I haven’t seen it much since I bought it for you.”

“I haven’t taken it off since I left,” Tori replied. “It’s a part of me now, just like you.”

Holly squeezed her hand and grinned, a smile that filled her whole face.

“So, this is San Francisco.” Holly swept her gaze around the airport as they started to walk again, striding towards the exit.

Tori nodded. “Yep, Fog City to its friends. On its behalf, I welcome you. What do you think of it so far?”

Holly glanced at her, the wheels of her case squeaking as she rolled it along. “So far, I think I might like it just fine.”

***

"So just how did Valentine take you leaving?" Tori asked.

"With a nonchalant roll of his eyes, like all good cats should. When I dropped him off at Dad and Sarah's, Elsie already had him strapped to her side by the time I left, so at least he's going to get a lot of attention over the next two weeks. I think Dad's a bit worried they might have to get a cat now, although I told him they can just borrow Valentine."

Holly was peering out the window of the apartment, backing on to Mission Dolores Park. Out the window, an array of locals were walking their dogs, sitting on benches and taking their day in their stride.

To them, it was just another day, whereas to Holly, it was momentous because she was finally in San Francisco. "It's lovely out here, I can see why you like it," she said. "It's like a movie set or something, with the park and the houses."

"It is at first, but you get used to it."

Holly turned and took Tori in her arms. "Are you attached to it yet? Still planning on coming home to London and to me?" Her stomach lurched as she said it — she knew that talk was still to come and she wasn't looking forward to it.

"Of course I am," Tori said, kissing her lips. "But we can talk more about that later, okay?"

Holly tried to read her body language, but she couldn't quite place it — perhaps it was going to take a while to get reacquainted, despite what she would have liked.

"Promise?"

"Promise," Tori said. "But you've got your photoshoot and we're leaving in less than an hour. You want to have a shower first?"

Holly nodded. Her clothes felt as if they were stuck to her body, the grime of the plane infiltrating into every fibre of her being. "That'd be great. Is it close by where we're heading?"

"Not too far, and we have the company's Uber account at our disposal, so just let me know when you're ready. If you think they arrive quick in London, you should see how they do it in the town it all began. I swear, there's an Uber driver for every person in this city, it's that good."

Tori took Holly's hand and pulled her towards the bedroom. They tumbled onto the bed and Holly held Tori close, kissing her lips, stroking her soft skin, feeling her heartbeat. "I've missed this, have I told you that?" Her skin hummed as it touched Tori's again, warming to the reconnection.

"Tell me again."

"Stop it, we're turning into a corny movie."

"You started it."

Holly squinted upwards, looking at the shelf above the bed. "What's that thing on the shelf?" She was referring to some kind of ornament — it looked like a fat Buddha, and she was pretty sure Tori hadn't become religious in the last six weeks.

"Not sure. Trudi looked it up and we decided it might

be a fertility statue of some sort, well at least it might according to Google."

Holly raised an eyebrow. "So you thought you'd adopt it because?"

Tori laughed, kissing her on the cheek. "No reason — I just liked the look of it and I think it'll bring me luck."

"In getting pregnant?"

Tori nudged Holly with her elbow. "Just in general, stupid."

"We can try getting pregnant in the shower now if you like?" Holly gave Tori a wink, holding up her right hand.

Tori winced. "I can't believe I'm saying this, but I don't think we have time."

"Not even a quickie? I promise to make you come in minutes?"

"And they say romance is dead," Tori replied, laughing. "I'd like it to be more than a quick fumble when we do. I haven't seen you in six weeks."

"Okay," Holly replied. "But just to be clear, you haven't gone off me, right?"

Tori shook her head. "No chance."

Holly nodded, satisfied for now, before rolling off the bed and starting to get undressed. "I'll just show you what you're missing," she said, tugging off her top, followed by her bra. "Is it how you remember?"

She had Tori's attention, her eyes glued to Holly's tall, slim frame.

"I've almost forgotten what you look like — it's a stunning view."

"You can transfer your adoration a little closer, if you like," Holly said, holding out a hand, her lopsided grin on her face.

Tori got up and ran her hands over Holly's naked breasts, before kissing them tenderly.

"Damn Trudi and her schedule," Tori said, stroking Holly's cheek. "I'll make it up to you later."

"You better," Holly replied, a shiver running down her body at Tori's touch. "Want to come and watch me, at least?"

"Try and stop me," Tori replied.

Chapter Sixteen

"Welcome, welcome, welcome!" Trudi said, even though they were 15 minutes late. Trudi wasn't about to tell them off though, seeing as Holly had just landed.

Trudi kissed Holly on both cheeks — at least, she pretended to, more kissing the air beside them than anything else.

Tori had noticed that about her friend of late: she didn't seem to have time for even the basics, like kissing her friends hello. She'd put it down to the stress of getting the business up and running, but she might need to have a word with her. Just because she was this close to la-la-land didn't mean Trudi had to turn into a lovey.

"How was your flight?" Trudi asked, whisking Holly's coat off and plonking her down in a chair, before ushering a make-up artist over. "Sorry to rush you, but we've only got a certain amount of time, so you being late has meant there's no time for pleasantries. We'll chat while Mimi works."

Mimi stepped forward, a tube of what looked like concealer and foundation in her left hand, cleansers in her right. She set to work on Holly straight away.

"It was fine, but I'm not feeling like I'm in the best shape of my life for a photoshoot." Holly flexed her neck and Mimi shot her a look. "Sorry," Holly said.

"You look great, and your hair looks amazing." Trudi ran her hand up the shaved side of Holly's hair like she was an object for general consumption.

Holly shot Tori a look.

Tori simply shrugged, raising both eyebrows as she did so. Like she said, Trudi's behaviour of late was getting increasingly weird. Now, clearly, she thought she owned a piece of Holly as well as Tori.

"Anyway, Portia is readying the lighting. We're going for casual, old-school style, white T-shirt, leather jacket, face side-on to camera. You're going to look incredible, trust me. Portia is a photography genius."

"Are you not using the ones she already did in London?" Tori asked.

"Yes, but we want a variety of looks which is why we decided to get two sets of photos done. Then it's down to whatever makes the brand look best." Trudi gave Holly's arm a squeeze. "See you over there when Mimi's done and you look a million dollars."

Trudi skipped off, and Holly glanced over at Tori. "Has she been like this the whole time you've been here?"

"Pretty much. She thinks she's on a reality show and she has to play to camera the whole time. The other day, she called me sweetie."

"What did you say?"

"I called her Bubble and that shut her up."

Holly laughed and Mimi frowned. "Can you stop laughing so much while I'm doing this? A bit of talking's fine, but you're moving your face too much."

"Sorry," Holly said again, before turning to Tori. "Go and annoy Trudi, I need to concentrate."

Chapter Seventeen

"That photo should be your wedding invite; it's perfect." They were in a bar around the corner from where the photoshoot had happened, and Trudi had just ordered a round of martinis to celebrate Holly's arrival. "I mean it, it's to die for."

"Only, it doesn't have Tori in it," Holly replied.

"We can Photoshop her in," Trudi said after a moment, before snapping her fingers. "Actually, you know what, Portia's coming back to do the launch party on Thursday — we'll get some shots of you two there. Think of it as my engagement gift to you." Trudi grinned, more than a little pleased at her cleverness.

"That would be lovely," Tori replied. "The ones they took today were beautiful, though — you're going to be a lesbian dating superstar."

"Just what I was after," Holly replied, smiling. She took a sip of her drink and recoiled. "Yikes, these are strong. I forgot we're in America."

"You get used to it," Trudi said, waving a hand. "Apart from Shauna, who was wiped out the first two weekends after imbibing one too many cocktails. She soon learned her lesson though, didn't you, sweetheart?"

"I did," Shauna said, nodding. "I only have to get a crashing headache four times in a row before the reality sinks in."

"So, what are your plans now you're here? I hear you brought a friend?" Trudi asked.

Holly nodded, checking her phone. "She flew out a few days ago — she should be here any minute if she managed to follow the instructions I sent her. Which is a big if with Kerry.

"Apart from that, my plans are to see the city, eat some food, come to your launch party, go to a Giants game and spend time with my gorgeous fiancée when you let her off the leash."

"She better be a good girl, then," Trudi said, grinning at Tori, before turning back to Holly. "You've arrived a few months too late to go to a lesbian bar — they're all closed now."

"I know, I can't believe that. I feel like we should go to the Lexington and have a photo taken in homage."

"We can do," Tori said. "And about that Giants game — it's not baseball season. So I've booked us basketball tickets instead, I hope that's okay."

"Perfect," Holly said, kissing Tori on the lips. "I just want to go to a game of some sort."

"You'll love basketball, it's great," Trudi said. "And maybe you can come back again while Tori's here for a Giants game later in the year — especially seeing as she's probably going to be here a while longer now."

Holly's body stiffened at Trudi's words and she glanced across at her girlfriend, cocking her head as if asking a question. "Really? News to me."

"And news to me," Tori added, at pains to show Holly that it was. What was Trudi doing? They hadn't discussed *anything* yet, so she was way out of line.

Tori's blood thickened and anger twisted in her veins, and it took all her efforts to keep a lid on it, but she managed it.

For now.

She didn't need this, not on the day Holly had arrived.

Holly's brow was furrowed and she wasn't looking at Tori as Trudi kept talking.

"It's not *really* news, is it?" Trudi said. "I mean, a three-month stint was unlikely, and it looks like we've got money for at least a year, probably two. So the door's open." She nudged Holly with her elbow. "Might be time to start packing your bags!"

It took all Tori's effort not to reach over and cuff Trudi round the ear: these larger measures were making her mouth loose again.

Instead, Tori reached over and gripped Holly's arm to get her attention. "This is the first I've heard of it, believe me," Tori said, holding Holly's gaze, hoping it was telling her all she needed to know.

Then she turned to Trudi. "And you," she said, with a finger wag. "Holly only just arrived today and we haven't even discussed anything — so you think you could keep your musings to yourself till we have?" Tori's patience with Trudi had just about run dry.

In response Trudi clapped her hand over her mouth. "Sorry, me and my big mouth. I keep forgetting you only just got here today — it's all the images of you everywhere, I feel like you're with us all the time."

She grinned at Holly, and the thought crossed Tori's mind that maybe she was trying to cause issues between her and Holly? Over the last six weeks, she'd hardly been their cheerleader.

The blood had drained from Holly's face and she looked confused and hurt. She was grinding her teeth, which was never a good sign.

Tori didn't blame her, but she had to press home to Holly that her and Trudi hadn't talked yet — and they wouldn't without Tori discussing it with Holly first.

Tori was just about to say something when she was interrupted by the arrival of Kerry, looking freshly laundered and ready for a night out.

She put her hand on Holly's shoulders, who twisted in her seat and grinned, getting up to give her friend a hug.

"Long time no see," Holly said.

Kerry held her at arm's length. "What's it been — three days?"

"Too long, clearly." Holly pulled over another seat for Kerry and the group shuffled around the table to make space for her.

"Hello, Tori. Did you miss me?" Kerry stooped over and planted a kiss on Tori's cheek, a familiar cheeky grin plastered on her face.

Yes, Tori remembered it well, even after not seeing her for two years. "Every minute of every day, of course," Tori said, holding out an arm and giving Kerry an awkward hug. Despite her reservations, Tori was going to be welcoming to Kerry, for Holly's sake. "It's good to see you."

"You, too," Kerry replied, sitting down and smoothing down her jeans. "And you and Holly are engaged now. Who would have thought after all these years?"

Tori shrugged. "Just goes to show, doesn't it?"

"It does — there's someone out there for everyone, even you!"

Strike one. Tori took a deep breath and gave Kerry her best smile. "Maybe even for you, Kerry, imagine that!" She could give as good as she got.

Kerry nodded, rubbing her hands together. "Maybe even here in San Francisco, with the help of Babe Magnet."

"Well apparently after that article, Tori had numerous offers from assorted crazies," Holly spat. "Perhaps she still has their numbers."

Ouch.

Clearly Trudi's announcement still needed smoothing over — not that Tori was surprised. She exhaled, swallowing back a mix of bile and tears that were bubbling in her throat. It was as if their emotional reunion today had never happened, wiped out by a casual comment from Trudi's mouth.

Oblivious, Kerry laughed. "Sounds ideal."

"Good to meet you," Trudi said, offering her hand to Kerry. "I'm Trudi, founder of Babe Magnet."

And general shit-stirrer, Tori wanted to add, but didn't.

"Co-founder," Shauna added, leaning forward.

Kerry shook their hands. "Nice to meet you both."

"And if you do find love through Babe Magnet, we'd be happy to feature you," Trudi added. "Anyway, go grab yourself a drink — just quote tab 776. And you're officially invited to our big Babe Magnet launch party on Thursday, too. Expect plentiful women and flowing champagne."

"Tonight is getting better by the second." Kerry pushed out her chair and stood up, stretching as she did so, showing off her lean midriff as her black top rode up her body.

Shauna raised an eyebrow and downed her martini. "I'll come with you," she said, glaring at Trudi as her girlfriend draped her gaze over Kerry.

"Me, too," Holly added, scraping her chair back, shooting Tori a look etched with hurt. "I could do with a stiff drink, that's for sure."

Kerry slung an arm over Holly's shoulders. "You're in the right country for that."

Chapter Eighteen

Holly was full of booze, emotion and jet lag, never a good combination. She was pressed against the outside wall of the bar they'd been in, her features slumped, a scowl on her face. Tori would have loved to know what was going on in Holly's head, even though she was pretty sure it was dark and stamped with foreboding.

Tori, on the other hand, had switched to water after a while, and now she was just exhausted from the whole evening.

Trudi, Shauna, Kerry and Holly had got steadily drunker as the night had gone on, and Tori had watched with a sinking heart. Far from being the evening she'd anticipated — one of reconnecting with her lover — she'd just had a sideline view, watching as the volume went up and the sense evaporated into thin air.

Now the court jesters had departed, there was just sourness coating the air. Plus, she was pretty sure Holly hated her.

"I thought you said there was an Uber on every corner in this town. Where the hell are they tonight? I can hardly keep my eyes open and I can't believe you gave Kerry the cab before us." Holly was slurring her words to the point of them being almost incomprehensible.

Tori gave her a look. "She was going home on her own, I thought it was the polite thing to do. And as she's *your* friend, I thought it was what you'd want to do, too."

Holly harrumphed, clutching her leg before sliding down the wall and sitting on the pavement.

Tori slid down next to her, shivering as she did so: it was cold in San Francisco tonight in more ways than one.

She blinked slowly as she glanced sideways at Holly, taking in the extra-wide streets, the taller trees, the thicker air.

Everything seemed alien to her right now, especially Holly, even though she was sitting next to her. Were they drifting apart or was this just getting used to each other again and what she should expect? Her mind clouded with doubt as the chill of the pavement seeped into her buttocks.

Holly was rubbing her leg.

"Is it hurting?"

Holly shrugged. "It always does at night."

"Poor you."

Holly blew out a breath and it swirled in the air around her.

"Not very Californian, this weather, is it?"

Holly shook her head. "And it smells like drains."

"You get used to it," Tori replied. She ran a hand up and down Holly's arm.

Holly stared at her hand, but didn't respond.

"I haven't told Trudi I'm staying for a year, just so we're clear." Tori sighed as she spoke.

Holly twisted her head, squinting as she did. Was she trying to focus her wobbly world? Probably.

"Nothing's that clear to me right now," she said. "I mean, I've just landed and then Trudi tells me you're not coming home. You didn't even do me the courtesy of letting me know."

"Trudi has a big mouth and she makes things up." Tori was trying to keep calm, but it wasn't easy. Plus, Trudi had been stirring all evening and Holly wasn't thinking straight, so she should try to steer the conversation away from contention. "Of course I'm coming home."

"But are you putting a date on it?"

Anger rose in Tori as she picked up her phone and glared at the screen. She hadn't asked for any of this: she hadn't even had the conversation with herself.

"Well that's just charming," Holly spat.

Tori glanced up, frowning. "What is?"

Holly placed her palms on the floor and pushed herself upwards, getting onto her knees before standing up straight. She staggered slightly and gripped her leg before she continued.

"I'm asking about our future and you're checking your phone!" Her voice had gone up an octave and was beginning to flail in the air, like it was drunk, too.

"I was checking to see if our cab was nearby!" Tori said, her tone clipped.

"Have I been out of your life for so long? Did it only take six weeks for you to leave me behind?" She scowled, looking down at Tori who was now scrambling to her feet. "Did you go out with any of those women who contacted you? Did you sleep with any of them?"

Tori grabbed Holly's arms. "Stop it! Just stop it." Her voice split the air like a gun shot.

It had the desired effect: Holly's vitriol was stopped in its tracks and she shut up.

"You're drunk and jetlagged and you're talking shit." Tori paused, gasping for breath like it was in short supply. "No I didn't go out with any of those women, and the only woman I've shagged in the past six weeks is myself, numerous times. Happy?" Tori paused, but didn't wait for an answer.

"Trudi's been making noises about extending my stay to six months — that was *always* on the cards and honestly, I will be here till June. We *always* knew that was a big probability. Her and Shauna will stay for longer." She dropped one of Holly's wrists, but hung on to the other.

"And yes, I think Trudi would be happy if I did the same, but it's nothing I was going to decide till we'd spoken and I didn't want to do it over FaceTime — I wanted to do it in person."

Holly's face turned into one giant billboard of

contempt: it was so pronounced, Tori felt nauseous looking at her. How had it come to this?

"So you thought you'd wait till I was over here and then tell me you're not coming back?" Holly stabbed her chest with her index finger. "I'm planning our wedding or has that escaped your notice?"

"Of course not!" Tori replied. "You're being ridiculous. I was always coming back for that."

"Big of you."

Tori sighed, shaking her head. "You know what? I do want to have this conversation with you, but not when you're drunk — that's not ideal."

"Maybe it is ideal — maybe it's perfect. Because people tell the truth when they're drunk, don't they? Things come out exactly as they should do, no holds barred." Holly paused, looking Tori in the eye.

"So tell me — do you want to stay? Should I even be booking places for the wedding?" Holly started grinding her teeth again as she waited for an answer.

"I," Tori began, before pausing. She wanted to let Holly know that *of course* she should, but she wanted to get the words right, not make her even madder. Tori's face went through a gamut of emotions as she got her words in the correct order.

Only she clearly took too long, because it was Holly who spoke next, snarling as she did.

"You cannot be serious."

"I haven't given you an answer yet!" Tori said, her

carefully chosen words now sprawled on the floor as if they'd just been punched.

Careful wasn't what was needed right now: she needed to drum the message home to Holly, speak from the heart.

She opened her mouth to speak, but Holly got in first again.

"And that in itself speaks volumes!" Holly began pacing the pavement in circles, shaking her head vigorously. "Wow, this is really going to be a fun trip if I'm getting dumped on the first night here." She grabbed Tori's arm and held on tight. "I can't believe you'd do this to me." She was pounding her finger on her chest again. "Me! I'm your *best friend*."

Holly's face crumpled when she said that, which made Tori's heart splinter, before breaking in two.

Damn it, she had to do something and fast. This was spiralling out of control.

Tori clapped her hands loudly in front of Holly's face, which made Holly stagger left.

Tori caught her and held her in place. "Holly, *listen to me*. I am not dumping you, I am still your fiancée and we're still getting married. And I was going to talk to you about you moving out here for a year as *one option*. Delaying your plans for your course maybe, trying California for a year, and then we could both move back together." Tori sighed, still holding Holly in place. "And on a sidewalk—"

"—pavement," Holly interrupted.

"Sidewalk, it's in America," Tori replied. "On a sidewalk at 1am is not when I was imagining having this conversation, but having it we are. But I'd still prefer to have it again, say, over breakfast or something like that." Tori paused. "When you're a bit more rational and a lot less drunk. And that's Trudi's fault, too, for buying all those shots."

"Seems like it's very convenient that everything's Trudi's fault. What about you taking some responsibility for your own life?"

"I was! I am!" Tori threw up her hands now. "It's why I wanted to wait till you got here, like I said."

Holly opened her eyes wider in a bid to stay upright and focus. It wasn't easy. "All I want to know is this. I've booked the wedding for October and I thought you'd be home by then — you hadn't told me otherwise. So, will you be?"

"But that's why I wanted to talk to you, to talk things through before you send out any invites or put down any deposits."

"You know I've already put down a deposit."

"Is it refundable?"

"No it's not bloody refundable!" Holly shook her hands free and threw her arms up in the air, circling the pavement again. "Are you having second thoughts about us getting married? Because if you are, I'd rather know sooner rather than later. All the evidence is stacking up, isn't it?"

Holly shook her head, raising her voice. "And I can't believe you're telling me this now. After you saw the venue with us and didn't say a word. After you knew I've booked it." She paused. "Even Kerry was starting to say nice things about you, but maybe she was right to be sceptical. Maybe it's true what they say: don't date your friends."

"Will you listen to me for five seconds, *please*? Stop ranting and *listen*!" Tori screamed the last word, before taking in where she was, taking a deep breath and trying to calm down.

On the opposite side of the road, a couple walking past picked up their pace. Tori didn't blame them — Holly and her looked crazy, but she didn't care. If she was going down, she was going in a blaze of glory.

"I didn't say anything because I wanted to talk to you in person. To test the water, to see where things stood. I was always still coming home to get married, but I don't want to live apart from you once we are — that's really important to me.

"Which is why I wanted to ask if you'd *consider* moving here — but just as a suggestion for us to talk about." Tori sagged as she clenched her jaw. "But then Trudi forced my hand and this *really* didn't go as planned."

"I guess it didn't. Then again, there really is no great way to tell your fiancée you don't want to marry them anymore."

Every sinew of Tori's body clenched tight: she wanted to scream, but she knew there was no point. Holly wasn't seeing things straight right now, so the best thing to do was to shut up and get her home. Any more chat wasn't going to do any good at all.

As if sensing that, right at that moment, their cab pulled up. Tori checked her phone, then squinted at the car number plate, before nodding.

"This is our car. Let's just get home, get some sleep and talk about this tomorrow."

"You have to work tomorrow with Trudi, who you share more of your life with anyway."

Tori took a deep breath, before exhaling. She just had to get home before screaming, that was all. "Tomorrow night, then."

"It's the launch party tomorrow night."

"Are you getting in or not?" the driver asked through his open window. "Only, I have more fares to pick up if you're not."

"Yes, we're getting in, aren't we?" Tori said, pushing Holly towards the car.

"I'm not getting in any car with you," Holly said, folding her arms across her chest like a toddler.

"Fine, shall I leave you here on the street in a strange city?" Tori didn't wait for an answer, instead pushing Holly towards the car and bundling her in. Tori was stronger than she looked sometimes.

She gave Holly a final shove across the back seat,

to some grumbling, before giving the driver the address of their flat.

Despite everything, as the car pulled away, she went to grab Holly's hand — but Holly pulled it away.

Tori sighed audibly. When she turned her head, Holly's eyes were already drifting shut.

What a night — but hopefully, with luck, they could sort this out in the morning.

Chapter Nineteen

"Thanks a lot for last night." Tori had a hand on her hip, feet apart. It was a stance that screamed 'don't fuck with me'.

She hoped Trudi was getting it because she was in no mood to be subtle this morning.

She hadn't slept well unsurprisingly, and she'd crept out this morning for their breakfast meeting with a possible advertiser, leaving Holly to catch up on her much-needed sleep. Her fiancée hadn't stirred an inch while she was getting ready.

"What did I do?" Trudi asked, sitting down at her desk and sipping her latte. She was massaging the side of her head, too, which Tori was sure had to be hurting.

"Telling Holly I'd be staying here for a year or two. *We* haven't even talked about that yet, but it didn't stop you opening your big gob, did it?"

Trudi opened her mouth to say something, then closed it. She swallowed before responding. "I… Wow, you caught me unaware. We just had a whole meeting and you were nice as pie to me in that."

"I'm a professional."

"You are," Trudi agreed, tapping her fingers on her desk. "Look, sorry if I spoke out of turn — I didn't mean anything bad by it, it just came out."

"Like things seem to be doing with you. Whether you meant it or not, Holly now thinks I want to stay here and not come home and marry her."

Trudi scrunched up her face. "From me saying one little thing?" She clicked her tongue stud on her teeth in the silence that followed. It was a habit that was grating on Tori this morning more than Trudi could possibly imagine.

"You told her I wasn't moving back!" Tori slumped down in the seat next to Trudi. "It wasn't just *one little thing*." She put the last three words in air quotes. "Look, I don't want an argument with you this morning — I already had one of those with Holly last night and frankly, I'm all argued out."

Tori paused, clenching her fingers into a ball before continuing. "What I need from you is to keep your mouth shut and let us work this out. I told you before that if I decide to stay longer, it has to be mine and Holly's decision, not yours. And it might be that the best thing for me is to go home and if that means losing my job, so be it."

Trudi studied Tori's face for a few moments. "Take all the time you need," she said, twisting in her chair. "I'm not planning on sacking you anytime soon."

"Glad to hear it."

"Do you have an inkling what you might want to do?"

"I don't know what I want, what's best for me." Tori paused. "I mean, for *us*."

Trudi raised an eyebrow.

"Slip of the tongue," Tori said, feeling her cheeks flush. She had been totally planning on telling Holly, they just hadn't had a moment to themselves since she landed. "Just no more shooting your mouth off, okay?"

"That's a tall order — Trudi keeping her mouth shut," Shauna said, leaning down to kiss her girlfriend. As she stood up, she took her Dodgers cap off and smoothed down her long hair, before replacing it.

"I promise, I won't open my mouth around Holly," Trudi assured Tori. "I will just smile and tell her how gorgeous she looks as the face of Babe Magnet. Because she does."

"She really does," Tori said, glancing down at the marketing material on her desk with her fiancée's face all over it. "She's so perfect."

And she was: now all Tori had to do was convey that to Holly without her girlfriend jumping down her throat again.

Girlfriend? *Fiancée.*

Damn, relationships were never easy, were they? "She's been here less than 24 hours and we've already had a massive row." Tori's whole body let out a sigh.

Shauna sat on the edge of Tori's desk, patting her on

the shoulder. "It's just getting to know each other again — these things happen. You'll be fine, you're Tori and Holly. You're invincible!"

"I like to think we are," Tori replied, her voice knotted with nerves.

"Could you work on that for the launch later?" Trudi chipped in. "Only, I'm announcing your engagement tonight, so it would help if you were talking to each other."

Tori spluttered. "God, I'd forgotten that," she said, putting her head in her hands. "I'm meant to be the blushing bride-to-be, aren't I?"

Trudi nodded. "You are," she said. "And you," she said, pointing at Shauna. "Don't forget to buy a Giants cap for the launch later. Or, at least, don't turn up in that Dodgers cap."

"I know — you told me this morning."

"We don't want all our hard work ruined by you supporting the wrong team, now do we?"

"We do not," Shauna replied. She looked at Tori. "You look tired."

"Thanks," Tori said. "I didn't sleep well, surprisingly."

"How was Holly last night by the way? She was pretty wasted when we all left."

Tori sighed. "Wasted would be the word. And now also convinced I don't want to marry her and want to stay here and frottage with American women."

"Frottage — you're so poetic sometimes. I would have just said fuck," Trudi replied, grinning.

"I don't want to frottage or fuck any of them, that's the point." Tori threw her head back in her chair and spun around. "Argh!" she said. "Women! Why do we do it to ourselves?"

"Can't live with them, can't live without them," Trudi said.

"Thank you, Dilbert," Tori replied.

"Listen, go into the meeting room and call Holly. Sort this out before tonight so you're all giddy with romance later for the big engagement reveal, okay?"

Tori rolled her eyes. "You're all heart, you know that?"

Shauna kissed the top of Tori's head. "What my girlfriend meant to say was, give Holly a call and work this out for you. Isn't that right?"

Trudi stood up and planted a kiss on Tori's cheek. "Of course. That's exactly what I meant for one of my oldest and best friends," she said. "Give her a call, tell her to stop being such a drama queen."

"I'm not sure that should be my opening gambit," Tori replied. "Anyway, we don't have time today, we have back-to-back meetings."

Trudi checked her phone. "You've got time now — there's over half an hour till the PR company are due. Call her now."

"What if she doesn't pick up?"

Shauna squeezed her shoulder. "She will, she loves you. But you won't know until you try."

Chapter Twenty

Holly opened another cupboard, but couldn't locate where they kept the bowls. Did they even have any bowls? Surely they must have if they'd been living here for nearly six weeks.

Then again, the fridge didn't have much in it apart from milk, Diet Coke and vodka, and the kitchen bore more of a resemblance to a dumping ground than a place to prepare food. The surfaces were covered in notepads, pens, make-up and takeaway leaflets, while the stove was so clean, she could see her face in it when she leaned over the top.

Holly held her head as she breathed out, nausea rising in her throat. She gripped the kitchen worktop and closed her eyes. Why had she drunk so much last night on an empty stomach and carrying jetlag? When would she learn?

She kicked herself mentally, and winced as she tried to recall getting home.

There was nothing there.

She remembered getting to the bar after the photoshoot,

Kerry turning up, Trudi telling her that Tori might not be coming home for another year, shots and then... nothing.

Shit, Tori wasn't coming home for another year? Was that right?

She walked quickly into the bedroom and grabbed her phone, dropping onto the unmade bed, now cold. She swung her legs up and put her head on Tori's pillow: Holly breathed in, smiling.

Until the room began to spin and her nausea rose.

Ugh.

She swung her legs back to solid ground and leaned her head between them.

She needed to eat and there was nothing in the flat — she wasn't surprised. This was Tori and Trudi, after all.

Tori had once told her they survived at university on Pot Noodles and Frosties, but Holly hadn't even seen those on her travels through the kitchen.

She sat up and checked through her phone: no incriminating photos, just a message from Tori this morning: 'Hope you're not feeling too bad babe, text me when you're up. Love you. X'

Had Tori and her had a fight? She had a nagging suspicion they had, but she couldn't remember any details.

She rubbed her eyes and her gaze wobbled. Her phone needed charging, so she plugged it into Tori's charger beside the bed.

She really needed some food and some coffee. There were cafes on the main street, so she should go there —

they'd have what she needed. Holly made a decision and got to her feet.

She strode back through the lounge and into the hallway, picking up the spare keys Tori had left for her on the hook by the door. She patted her jeans: she had her wallet, that was all she needed. She shrugged on her coat and stamped her feet, feeling the chill in the hallway already. As she turned the key in the lock, her phone began to ring in the bedroom.

She stopped momentarily: should she rush back in? No, her need for coffee was greater. She'd have breakfast and then call whoever it was back after that.

Holly pocketed the keys and made her way to the lift down the hallway.

* * *

'Hey — where you at? I've got meetings all day and we need to chat. Text me. X'

'I was just getting breakfast and much needed coffee. Feel like shit. Where are your pills? X'

'There's some in my bedside table — Advil. Take two, drink water, I suspect you need it. X'

'You're going through to voicemail — where are you? And daytime telly over here is shit by the way. X'

'I just tried you — where were you? I'm in meetings all day. Will try you again at 5. X'

'I was in the shower — feeling marginally better. X'

'Hey, meeting ran over and we need to get to the venue.

I guess I'll just have to meet you there. I'll WhatsApp you the address — you can walk it from the flat. X'

'Okay. I miss you. Did we have a fight last night? I don't remember much.'

'Yeah, we did. Where's my kiss on the end of the text? X'

'Sorry. Xxxx' Pause. 'Are we okay?'

'We'll talk later, but yes, we're fine. And remember, Trudi's telling everyone we're engaged tonight. X'

'She is? X'

'Yup. X'

'Do I need to dress up? X'

'You're the face of Babe Magnet. X'

'That's a yes then. Are you in a meeting right now? X'

'Uh-huh. X'

'Are you texting under the table? X'

'Uh-huh. I have to go — see you at 7?'

'Can't wait.'

'Kiss? X'

'Sorry! Xxxxxxxxxxxxxxxxxxxxxxxxxxxxxxxxxxx'

Chapter Twenty-One

The launch party was in full swing, with press, local businesses, prominent lesbians and all manner of friends invited. Tori was amazed at how many people had turned up, but then, it was free booze and she'd employed the services of a PR firm to rustle up bodies.

Looking around the room, it seemed that the great and the good of the lesbian scene were here: she'd been studying photos and names as if she was in *The Devil Wears Prada*, and had already talked to the owners of several prominent lesbian websites and magazines.

Now she cast her gaze around the room searching for Holly, but that wasn't hard. One whole side of the room was taken up with her face on a giant screen, and there were smaller, more discreet versions all around the room. She was used to it, but she was sure Holly would be a little freaked out.

What's more, Tori had a glass of champagne in her hand, being given out for the upcoming toasts — one of which was going to be for their engagement.

She couldn't put a finger on how she was feeling,

but it wasn't how she *thought* she should be feeling about announcing their union to the world. That was probably because she still hadn't had a chance to speak to Holly properly yet, to talk about their future. She'd make time this weekend, but tonight they were just going to have to style it out.

Tori jumped as a hand landed on her shoulder: she turned to see Holly smiling at her. She had on her red velvet jacket and some black trousers, and she looked every inch the lesbian model. The hot, gorgeous lesbian model, and her fiancée.

You'd never know she'd been on the sidewalk shouting at her less than 24 hours ago, but that was testament to the body's power of restoration, along with Holly's make-up skills. Her eye shadow and lipstick were on-point, and her lashes were curled to perfection.

"You ready to be engaged all over again?" Holly asked, coming in for a kiss but missing her mouth slightly.

Tori smiled: they weren't firing at 100 per cent just yet, but that was something she could change. "As I'll ever be."

Just as Tori said that, a hush fell across the room as Trudi got on stage with Shauna, grinning at the crowd.

"Welcome everyone to the launch of Babe Magnet, the brand new LBQ app for meeting like-minded women!"

Cheers and whistles from the crowd, and then Trudi went on to tell them how it started as a kernel of an idea over breakfast one morning, and look at them now.

"So thank you for being here and celebrating with us!" Trudi held up her glass of champagne. "To the success of Babe Magnet!" The crowd toasted the app, and Trudi waited for the chat to dim before carrying on.

"And if you'll indulge me, I have one more announcement to make." She put her hand up over her eyes, as if shielding them from the sun. "Tori, are you out there? And Holly? Can you come up?"

Tori grabbed Holly's hand and they walked up on the stage, to huge applause and cheers. Tori tried to ignore the stiffness in Holly's body, but it wasn't easy.

"I thought this would be the perfect time also for everyone to raise a glass to my good friend and key part of the Babe Magnet team, Tori Hammond. Because just before she flew out to work with us, she got engaged to her girlfriend, Holly Davis — so they never got an engagement party."

She turned to the pair, holding up her glass again. "So Tori and Holly, here's to you both, may you have a long and happy life together and many congrats on your engagement." She paused, holding up her glass to the crowd. "To Tori & Holly!"

More cheers, and Tori couldn't help but grin. All these women so happy for them made her believe in love all over again. She needed that tonight.

Tori stepped off the stage still holding onto Holly: after last night, she was holding on tight, not leaving anything to chance.

"Shall we get a drink?" Tori asked as a woman patted her on the back, telling her congratulations. She smiled her thanks as she carried on walking.

"Sounds perfect," Holly said, squeezing her hand.

Tori arrived at the bar and ordered two of the house cocktails, a pungent mix of gin and something pink.

Holly stroked the small of Tori's back and the intimate connection made her smile. She took the drinks from the bartender, putting a tip in the jar before she turned around.

When she did, Holly kissed her, and this time, the kiss connected first time. Relief surged in Tori's body.

"Hey, engaged lady," Holly said, her eyes reflecting the smile on her face.

"Hey yourself."

Holly still had a hand on her back. "You enjoying your engagement party?"

"We're very popular," Tori replied, with a gentle laugh.

"I know. All these people who want to say congrats, look at your ring, celebrate with us."

"But you haven't got a ring yet." Guilt rose up through Tori. She'd meant to do that, but what with the launch and everything else going on, she'd clean forgotten.

But Holly just shrugged, giving her a grin. "Don't worry about that," she said. "Let's just enjoy our engagement party, shall we? Free booze and food, along with tons of guests to share it with." She swept her hand around the room. "And look, you know at least ten of them."

"Don't exaggerate."

"Okay, seven."

"At a push." Tori paused, before catching Holly's eye. She wanted to be happy, but their argument was still playing on her mind. "I just want to make sure everything's alright after last night. We had a big fight."

Holly gave her a sad smile. "I don't remember much of it, only you saying you might not come home."

Tori shook her head. "That's not right — we need to talk."

"And we will — just not now." Holly squeezed her hand. "Just hang in there tonight, and we can sort everything out tomorrow." She paused, searching Tori's face. "Just one thing: you do still want to marry me, right?"

Gut-wrenching fear flushed through Tori, and she nodded her head with all her might. "Of course," she said, putting a hand to Holly's face. They were in a crowded bar full of people, but right now, the spotlight was on them, just the two of them. "Marrying you is the one thing in life I'm completely certain about."

Holly's face softened at her words. "That's all I needed to hear."

"Hello, young lovers!" a voice said, breaking the moment.

Tori turned to see Kerry standing next to her, looking… dare she say it, hot? There was something about Kerry these days, the way she was always smiling, her stance. She had a confidence about her that hadn't been there before.

She kissed them both hello, then held out a gift bag with what looked like a bottle of champagne in it.

"I got here just in time for the big announcement." Kerry was beaming as she spoke. "I even brought you a present," she said, offering Holly the bag. "Seeing as I wasn't there first time round, this is as good a second occasion as I could possibly imagine."

Holly took the bag from her and gave her a hug. "You didn't need to do that."

Tori shook her head. "No, you really didn't."

"Nonsense, it's a big deal. You're getting hitched!" Kerry gave Tori an exaggerated wink. "So how are the happy couple? Radiating with love? Or hungover from last night?" She blew out a breath. "I know I was a bit hanging this morning."

Tori glanced at Holly, and Holly did the same to her.

'On edge' would be Tori's answer, but she couldn't say that. She couldn't say that she wanted to whisk Holly away and have it be just the two of them, to talk, to make love, to reconnect.

"Fine, we're good," was her actual reply.

"Wow, bowl me over with your enthusiasm," Kerry replied. "I was hoping for some gushing declarations of undying love, but I can see I may have come to the wrong place."

Tori didn't think she could feel more ill at ease, but it wasn't Kerry's fault — she was just being chatty.

But then, saved by the bell, Melissa arrived, walking up and giving Tori a shy wave. Tori was so pleased to steer the attention away from them, she threw her arms around her friend, giving her a bear hug. If Melissa was shocked by her enthusiasm, she didn't say anything, instead simply smiling as Tori released her.

"So glad you could make it," Tori said, relief flooding through her as she turned to Holly. "This is Melissa from The Chronicle — remember I told you we met at the press launch and went to brunch together?"

Holly stuck out a hand and Melissa took it. "Of course, lovely to meet you."

"You, too," Melissa replied. "And congrats on your engagement — I didn't realise she was going to do a big announcement at the launch."

"You know Trudi," Tori said with a rueful smile.

Kerry interrupted, holding out a hand to Melissa. "Nice to meet you, I'm Kerry."

"Sorry, this is our friend from London," Tori added.

"Lovely to meet you," Melissa said, her eyes sweeping over Kerry as she shook her hand. "You didn't tell me you had a friend visiting."

"I'm actually living here now," Kerry said, taking Melissa's arm. "Want me to tell you about my move while we get a drink?"

Melissa glanced at Tori as if seeking permission, but only took a few seconds to nod at Kerry. "I'd love to," she said, as Kerry steered her away.

Tori watched them go, smiling at their backs before turning to Holly. "You know, you can level a lot of things at Kerry, but one thing you can never say is she lets the grass grow under her feet. She sees what she wants and she goes for it."

"Good thing most people aren't like that, isn't it? Or else dating services like Babe Magnet would never exist and you wouldn't have a job."

"Very true." Tori paused. "So here's to not everyone being like Kerry."

* * *

Three hours later and the volume had gone up several levels, just as the sobriety of the remaining party-goers had gone down.

The DJ was pumping out old-school classics, and Tori, despite her earlier misgivings, was actually having a good time, and had even shared a dance with Trudi. Going back to what they'd always done as friends before working together had felt good; easy to slip into like a well-worn pair of jeans.

Trudi's laugh rang out around the room, and Tori turned to where her colleague was standing by the enormous image of Holly's face along with Shauna, Melissa and Kerry. Kerry said something, and the other two laughed.

Tori made her way over to them, casting her gaze around for her fiancée: she spotted her chatting to a couple of women she didn't recognise on the other side of the room. She watched as Holly nodded at something one of the women said, and a swell of love and pride engulfed her.

No matter how strange their first couple of days had been, she was glad Holly was here with her, and that the night was nearly over so they could go home. Holly might be the living embodiment of Babe Magnet, but she was also hers.

"Hey," Tori said as she arrived at Trudi's side.

Trudi turned and slung an arm over Tori's shoulder, kissing her cheek as she did. "Going great, isn't it?" she said, surveying the room. The crowd had thinned out, but there was still a respectable number on the dance floor and beyond.

"Here's to us, and here's to Babe Magnet," Trudi said, holding up her glass.

Tori held up her empty hands. "I'm out of booze."

Trudi gave her a look. "I was just saying to these guys about the power of Babe Magnet. Just think: somewhere out there, there's probably two lesbians having sex because of us." Trudi folded her arms across her chest, a satisfied grin on her face.

"If there are, our work here is done," Tori replied, smiling.

"No! Our work is to get as many lesbians having as much sex as possible." Trudi paused, clutching her chin. "You think I should change our strapline from 'meeting like-minded women'?"

Tori shook her head. "I'd stick with what we've got."

Trudi pouted. "Spoilsport." She paused. "Anyway, we're going to take the party back to ours, and Melissa and Kerry are coming, too." She checked her watch. "This finishes up in 30, so we'll head back then?"

Tori nodded her head. "Sure, sounds good," she said, glancing at Melissa as Kerry stroked her back.

Melissa gave her a grin. "You never told me what a charmer your friend was," she said.

Tori laughed, then realised Melissa wasn't joking. "I never knew," she said, glancing at Kerry.

Chapter Twenty-Two

Tori was staring up at the ceiling when Holly stirred beside her. She turned and gave her a kiss on the temple, before resuming her solitary thoughts.

"What you thinking about?"

Tori paused for a second too long. "Our wedding," she said, eventually. "What it's going to be like walking down the aisle with you."

Holly rolled over and kissed her hand. "Nice try." She paused. "Now, what were you really thinking about?"

Tori glanced to her left. "I thought I styled that out pretty well."

"You nearly did."

"Hmmm," Tori said. "I was just thinking about Kerry — about her living in San Francisco at exactly the same time as me. What are the chances?"

"She had plans to come to the US way before you did," Holly said. "Or maybe she secretly fancies you and *that's* why she's here." Holly put a hand over her mouth, before rolling on top of Tori and kissing her. "Oh my god, it makes perfect sense now!"

Tori rolled her eyes, running her hand under Holly's T-shirt and up her bare back.

Holly wriggled at Tori's touch, her body revelling in what it had been denied for weeks.

"If Kerry secretly fancies me, I'll run naked through the streets of San Francisco, okay?"

"Almost worth getting her to lie," Holly replied, staring into Tori's eyes.

She'd always wished her best friend from uni and Tori would get on, but they never had. Somehow, they'd always rubbed each other up the wrong way, always been a little jealous of each other when it came to her.

Holly knew it was because when it came down to it, they were so similar, but it didn't make it any easier for her to mediate between them. She'd hoped that the passing of time would ease relations between them, and she was still hopeful.

"I don't think it's Kerry you need to worry about, anyway. From what I've seen, your own friends are doing a bang-up job of sabotaging us — Kerry doesn't have to do a thing."

Tori exhaled. "You might be right. Trudi is pressing all our buttons right now."

"She is. And I know you've never got on with Kerry, but now she's here, you think you could try? For me? Because it'd be nice if she knew someone who lived here."

As if to drive home her point, Holly pressed her lips to Tori's.

Tori looked pleasingly punch-drunk when she pulled away.

"Kerry can look after herself," Tori said eventually.

"You know what I mean."

Tori banged her teeth together, before rolling Holly off her and exhaling. "For you, you know I will. I promise. It's not going to be easy, but she's not going anywhere and neither am I, so yes, I'll try."

"Good." Holly paused. "Because I'm asking her to be my witness."

Tori's breathing stilled momentarily, before restarting. "Makes sense I suppose," she said. "She's one of your best friends after all."

"She is."

Tori sat up then, before twisting around. "Or you could ask Cheryl?"

"Cheryl? I wouldn't think about asking her." Holly and Cheryl had drifted in the past couple of years despite being close friends at university.

"Your mum?"

"I'm not asking my *mum*," Holly said, sitting up next to Tori now. Was Tori mad? Who asked their mum to be their witness?

"Look, she's not in our lives *all* the time, so just try to get on with her when she is, that's all I'm asking. And a witness at a wedding is no big deal. She's going to be there anyway."

Tori's shoulders went up and down as she sighed.

"You can stop being such a drama queen anytime soon," Holly added. "You'd think I was asking some despot to be my witness."

Even Tori had to smirk at that. "Fine, Kerry's your witness — no problem. And I'll try to see the better side of her from now on, too."

"Glad to see you're mastering the art of compromise even before we're married." She put an arm around Tori's shoulders.

"I'm just full of surprises, aren't I?" Tori paused. "One thing though: why did she have to hook up with Melissa?"

Holly let out a low, hollow laugh as she flopped down on the bed. "How's that 'seeing the best side of Kerry' going?"

Tori smiled now, too. "Give me time, I can't just flip a switch and boom, I'm a Kerry-lover!"

"No, we'll leave that privilege to Melissa," Holly replied with a grin. "Anyway, who's your witness?"

Tori rubbed her head at those words. "I dunno, I haven't really thought about it."

"You surprise me."

"I've been busy!" Tori said, resting her head on Holly's right breast. "But I'll give it some serious thought now I have a bosom for a pillow."

"Everybody needs one, apparently."

"So I heard." Tori kissed Holly's breast, then rolled over. "I dunno — probably Trudi. She's my Kerry, isn't she?"

"She is," Holly replied. "So no dissing my choice now, okay?"

"Point taken," Tori said. "I don't want to argue with you anymore. We seem to have been disagreeing with each other since you landed. I'm exhausted."

"And things still aren't sorted, are they?" Holly winced as she spoke. "I'm sorry if I was out of line the other night, but I don't remember much."

"It doesn't matter. The key thing was, Trudi would like me here for longer than six months. Possibly a year, maybe longer. So I was going to talk to you about what to do. Whether I say yes, whether I come home, or whether you move here for a year and delay your course." Tori moved her top lip one way, the bottom one the other. "What do you think?"

Holly looked up to the ceiling. "You still want to get married this year?"

"I do — of course I do."

"There's no 'of course' about anything anymore."

"There is — there totally is."

"But you might want to stay longer?"

Tori took a deep breath, before nodding her head. "Only if it works for both of us. I might still be back by June, but it might extend another couple of months, I can't say for sure. But I might have killed Trudi by then if she keeps opening her big mouth—"

"—not if I get there first—" Holly said, thinking very unkind thoughts about Tori's witness.

"—so it's all up in the air." Tori paused, then wrapped both arms around Holly, holding her tight. "Babe, in an ideal world, I'd be home in June and we'd be married in October in Miles's big gay mill house."

Holly sighed. "It was perfect you know," she said, her voice wobbly.

"It looked it. But this is our wedding, and I feel like I'm not part of it. You are, your mum is, Sarah is, hell even Kerry knows more about it than me. I feel a little… cut off."

Holly gave her a sad smile. "That's the last thing I want. But if you look at it another way, it'll all be a surprise on the day. It's like an episode of *Don't Tell The Bride*, but we're paying for it."

"So long as you haven't booked us a wild west or sci-fi wedding."

"Damn. Better put a stop on the Chewbacca outfits, then." Holly paused. "You are stupid, you know that? I'm only doing all this so we can move things along, get married when we planned. But if it's stressing you out, we can postpone it. I don't want you to be dreading your own wedding or feel like you're missing out. The main thing I want to do is marry you, and I don't care when that is, okay?"

She kissed Tori's lips, glad to feel the connection again. "I mean, the mill house is booked and I've told a fair few people, so October would be preferable, but if we have to move it, we do." She blew out a long breath. "So long as you're paying."

Tori untangled herself still holding Holly's hand. "But whether we get married in October or we get married further down the line: would living out here be something that interests you? Because one thing I've realised in the past six weeks is that whatever city I'm in, I want you with me. It's not a home without you, wherever I am."

Holly's stomach rumbled: here was the question she'd tossed around in her mind, wondered aloud about herself. Could she live here?

"I don't know. There's my family, Valentine, my course. I mean, if I started that, I couldn't leave it." She'd already begun to think of what life might be like when she was a student again, Tori returning, them both embarking on new ventures. Was it something she could do in America?

"You could postpone it."

"I could, but what would I do over here?"

"I'm sure we could find something."

Holly exhaled. "And there was me thinking this visit was going to be relaxing. I didn't realise we were going to make some life-changing decisions, too."

Tori gave Holly a sad smile. "I'm hoping it will be relaxing once we get all the life choices out the way." She paused. "Just think about it. We don't have to decide right now, but roll it around your brain, see what you think."

"I think I'm probably going to say no, because I wouldn't have anything to do here. I don't mind visiting, but if I was living here, I'd need a purpose."

"I know. But just sit with it for now, okay? For me?"

Holly nodded. "Sure — for you." She leaned over and kissed Tori. "It's never straightforward being your girlfriend, is it?"

"Fiancée," Tori corrected. "And no, I could never be accused of being boring." She paused, looking into Holly's eyes. "Are you bored of me being unboring?"

Holly laughed. "A little. Boring can be good." But she'd known what she was signing up for when she got Tori: a life less ordinary. She'd known it all along, so to start complaining now would seem a little churlish. "But even though you're unboring, I still love you."

Tori's eyebrows shot up and she smiled. "You do?"

"I do," Holly said, kissing Tori's lips.

"And I love you, too."

Holly got goosebumps all over her body as she responded to Tori's words. "So when we're making these life decisions, let's not forget that, okay? We love each other and we want to be together, and those are the two most important things, right?"

Tori nodded. "Absolutely."

"And your breasts are the third," Holly said, a smile creasing her face as she lowered her mouth to them. "I could kiss these all day long," she said, doing just that.

"Don't let me stop you," Tori said, wriggling under Holly's touch.

Holly ran a hand over Tori's breasts. "No more talking." She raised herself up and applied her mouth to

Tori's right breast again. "I'd rather spend time doing this."

"Didn't your mother ever tell you it's rude to speak with your mouth full?"

Holly sucked Tori's nipple into her mouth before replying. "She did, but I'm a very rude girl, what can I tell you?"

"It's one of the reasons I'm marrying you," Tori replied, her voice catching in her throat as Holly encased her nipple with her hot lips again.

After a few minutes, Holly flicked her gaze up to Tori, who was focused on her with laser-like precision.

"You know, I brought along a new toy if you want to try it out."

Tori's eyes widened. "You did?"

"Uh-huh."

"Well, I wanted it to be special — and I guess introducing a toy would make it that."

Tori cupped Holly's face and brought it towards her, kissing her on the lips before slipping her tongue into her mouth.

Holly's senses were a jumbled mess when they eventually broke apart. "I take it that means, 'go ahead and strap up, Holly'?"

Tori looked into Holly's eyes. "I think those are the most sexy words you've ever said to me."

"Better than 'would you like me to cook you a delicious steak'?"

Tori cocked her head. "Fuck me, then cook me a steak, and that would be my perfect day."

"Ha!" Holly said, kissing her again, before jumping off the bed and rummaging in her suitcase for the dildo and harness.

"Were you secretly hoping they'd stop you at customs and inspect your case?" Tori said, her head now leaning on a bent elbow, a sly grin on her face.

Holly turned around, black leather harness in hand. "Of course, why wouldn't I be?" She walked back to the bed and kissed Tori. "And your breasts look insanely gorgeous just sitting there, naked."

"You're breast obsessed."

Holly gave her a wink as she disappeared into the bathroom. "Yup."

Chapter Twenty-Three

In the bathroom, Holly glanced at herself in the mirror: her hair fell in front of her eyes and she swept it out of the way, before stepping into the black harness. She felt a gush between her legs and she pulled the straps up, before slotting the green silicon dildo into the hole. Then she pulled the straps tighter and glanced at her reflection.

She was standing tall and proud, ready for service. The leather was sitting snugly around her bum cheeks, the leather underneath damp from her own juices.

That was only going to intensify once she stepped through the door: her heart was already pounding in her chest at the thought of using a dildo with Tori — she wanted to make it perfect.

She gripped the sink and gave herself a hard stare as she took a deep breath, the dildo sticking out in front of her. "Ready?" she asked herself, before giving herself a nod in answer.

Hell yes, she was ready.

Holly stepped out of the bathroom and walked over to the bed, her green appendage leading the way.

Tori's eyes widened. "Whoa, that's pretty big. Was that the one we agreed on?" Tori gulped audibly.

Holly nodded. "It is." She paused, leaning over to kiss Tori, before kneeling on the bed. "But just see how you like it. We can go as slow as you want." Then she jumped back off the bed and sprang over to her case.

"What are you doing now?" Tori asked, impatience in her voice.

"Getting this," Holly said, holding up a tube of lube. "You won't be thanking me otherwise."

Tori grinned right back. "Wise woman," she said, springing up and crawling across the bed until she stopped, her mouth right in front of the dildo. "But before you lube up, which is a total turn-on, believe me, can I taste you first?"

A rush of endorphins swept through Holly's bloodstream, carrying her libido, shoulder-high. "Say that again," Holly said, her eyes clouding over with lust as she stared down at Tori's mouth so close to her silicon cock.

Tori, seeing the power she had, inched forward slightly and stuck out her tongue, circling the end of the toy.

Holly groaned: she knew it wasn't actually attached to her, of course she did, but it didn't stop a gushing between her legs as Tori played with her slowly, her gaze flicking up to Holly's face, before taking the toy in her mouth.

"Oh fucking hell," Holly said, gazing down at Tori as the dildo slid in and out of her mouth. For how Holly was feeling, Tori might as well have had her tongue on her pussy, swiping it upwards, down, round and round.

Then Tori pulled away, swinging her legs around until she was sitting on the edge of the bed in front of Holly. She manoeuvred her lover back to where she wanted her, then gave her a wink. "Go with me on this."

Holly couldn't get any words out right now even if she tried, so she just nodded, her breathing ragged and her clit pulsing. When she'd strapped up, she'd assumed she'd be the one driving: how wrong she'd been.

Tori grabbed both of her bum cheeks and gave them a squeeze.

Holly groaned again and thrust forward slightly. The ground shook and she smiled at Tori.

But now, Tori was looking up at her quizzically. "What was that?"

Holly's mind was clouded, misty. "What was what?" she said, waiting for Tori to continue, all her blood rushing down her body to her clit.

"Did you feel that shaking?"

"I thought it was us," Holly replied, her heart thumping in her chest. "Touch me, please." The final word was said in a whisper, pleading stamped through it.

Tori furrowed her brow, before refocusing and grabbing Holly by one cheek, reaching between her legs with the other hand and running her fingers through Holly's wetness.

"Oh yes," Holly said, looking down, seeing stars. All the pent-up sexual energy from the past six weeks was teetering on the edge, but Holly was determined to control it.

However, Tori wasn't going to make that easy. She grinned up at Holly and slipped one finger inside her, then a second, before slipping her lips around the silicon toy again, fucking and sucking Holly in one swift move.

It took every ounce of self-control Holly had not to fall to the floor in a heap — but if she did that, she knew her current scenario would come to a shuddering halt, and she didn't want that.

Her senses went into overdrive as she watched Tori's mouth work, and felt her lover's fingers slide in and out of her simultaneously. Waves of pleasure coursed through her as Tori picked up her pace, and Holly forced herself to keep her eyes open, never wanting this moment to end.

Right now, if Tori had asked her to drop everything and move here, she'd have agreed on the spot. Whatever else was happening in their lives, in this moment, Tori had her completely.

And then Holly felt the shudder again and it made her open her eyes wide. Was that tremor in her body or external? Because if it was her, this was now officially her new favourite position.

Outside the door, she heard furniture being scraped back and voices mingling, but she forced herself to shut it out. Right now, Tori was fucking her and that was what she wanted to focus on: she could feel her orgasm gathering steam, like an aria about to crescendo.

Tori knew it, too, because she wasn't stopping. Holly's heart was hammering in her chest as Tori's fingers pumped into her and her tongue swirled around the toy.

And then, there it was again. A slight rumbling, a shake, something not quite right.

Holly cast her gaze around the room. Everything seemed to be as it had been: her suitcase was still on the floor, their discarded clothes still on top of it. Her glass of water was still on her bedside table, along with her phone.

She shook her head.

Perhaps she was just imagining it.

Focus.

She glanced down to where Tori had her eyes open, licking her lips. Her fingers stilled. "What *was* that?"

"I'm not sure," Holly replied, breathless, her whole body purring. "But please don't stop."

Tori grinned up at her, sliding her fingers out and circling Holly's clit.

Holly's knees buckled. "Are you trying to kill me?" she whispered, as her body shuddered anew.

"How am I doing?"

"Outstanding," Holly replied, as Tori began fucking her again.

Holly thought she might pass out with desire: Tori was just too bloody perfect.

Holly ground down on Tori's fingers, and when Tori turned her focus to Holly's clit one more time, it tipped

Holly over the edge, her juices rushing, shouting out Tori's name.

Tiny glitter-bombs erupted in every pocket of Holly's being as her orgasm ripped through her again: damn, she loved this woman.

And she couldn't think of a more perfect moment this year than standing there in front of Tori, her orgasm shredding her senses, making everything around her deliciously incomprehensible.

Chapter Twenty-Four

Tori squeezed Holly's bum cheek, then she was on the move, scooting up the bed, hoping Holly would follow her. Because as much as she loved what they'd just done, now she wanted something more intimate, more together.

Tori wanted Holly on top of her, inside her, and she wanted to look into her smouldering eyes, into her soul, as she made love to her. And she hoped the look she was giving Holly signalled exactly that.

Holly still looked dazed, but she was on the ball, squeezing some lube from her travel-sized tube, before crawling up and over Tori like a tide, a sultry glare in her hooded eyes.

Tori wilted at the sight: she could already tell Holly was still in the zone and she was going to give her exactly what she wanted: to be filled and fucked by her fiancée.

Damn, right now, Tori was loving the letter F.

Holly sucked her nipples, left then right, the dildo sticky and wet on Tori's thighs, making her gush even more.

But Tori was in no mood to wait. "Babe," she said, looking into Holly's eyes. "I want you inside me, it's been way too long."

In response, Holly pressed down on Tori's lips, and the effect was instant, her tongue sliding deliciously into her mouth, the dildo still pressing down on Tori's pussy. She knew she was being schooled, but she pushed her hips up anyway, telling Holly what to do.

Eventually, Holly pulled back, licking up the side of her neck before reaching down with her hand and positioning the dildo over Tori.

Just watching Holly do that made Tori's insides pulse some more. She wanted them joined together, now more than *ever* before.

And then, Holly was pushing in gently, her eyes never leaving Tori.

In response, Tori spread her legs, opening up for her lover. And as the dildo edged into her bit by bit, she melted into the moment, not taking her eyes from Holly's penetrating gaze as she filled her. The moment was so encompassing, so intense, Tori almost forgot to breathe.

"You okay?" Holly asked, drawing back a little, and then sliding back in again with a shudder, her gaze never wavering.

Tori closed her eyes and blew a breath, then refocused on her lover. On her beautiful face, on her dazzling green eyes, the colour of love.

Was she okay? Tori had no idea. All she knew was,

she'd never felt anything like this in her entire life, with every nerve-ending in her body wired.

"I'm bloody exquisite," Tori whispered in reply.

It was all the invitation Holly needed, as she drew out again, then back in, slowly picking up a rhythm.

Tori rocked her hips in unison with Holly and crushed their lips together again, as if her life depended on it. This was everything she'd been missing; pure bliss, pure connection. As her lips slid across her lover's, and her pussy throbbed to Holly's beat, Tori floated away — she never wanted this moment to end.

And then, she shuddered so hard, she'd swear the room did, too. Had it? She opened her eyes, but all she saw was Holly above her, a blissed out look on her face. She crushed her lips back to hers.

Tori and Holly rocked as one, all other noises and lights faded out as Tori galloped towards her orgasm. And just when she thought she might need a little something else, Holly reached down and caressed her swollen clit.

That was all it took.

Tori's body imploded, her peripheral vision pixellating as her orgasm crashed through her, its spray lashing her outer edges, its centre lashing her soul. More followed, with Tori and Holly getting louder and braver with every wave, until Tori stroked Holly's leg and her lover slowed.

And then it was just the beat of her heart, the roar of her blood and Holly panting in her ear, her cheeks red with exertion, her smile as broad as her heart.

Tori moved her hips, and she pulsed again. She shut her eyes and let another wave of pleasure crash over her, before breathing out.

She trailed a hand down Holly's face, never losing her gaze. "You're pretty amazing, you know that?"

Holly's grin got even wider. "So are you," she whispered, before kissing Tori lightly.

Tori locked eyes with her lover, and she didn't think she'd ever felt this connected, this loved.

This was it: this was the reason they were destined for each other. How she wished she could hold on to this moment, and never let it go.

Chapter Twenty-Five

But the moment was soon spoiled by outside noise intruding on it: this time, someone was banging at their door.

Holly tried to make sense of the banging, but she was still inside Tori and their love-making had been off the charts. They were both still too frazzled by their orgasms to process the banging fully.

Until it happened again. "Guys, can I come in?" It was Kerry.

Tori was first to respond. "Hang on!" she said, moving, then stopping as she winced. "You're going to have to move first, babe," Tori said, giving her a peck on the cheek.

Holly eased out of Tori, her lover closing her eyes and groaning as she did, then Holly clambered off the bed as more banging ensued.

"Guys! Can I come in?" Jeez, Kerry was in a hurry today.

"Hang on Kerry, where's the fire?" Holly tried to shout, but her voice came out as a whisper.

But then, before Holly knew it, their door was thrown open and Kerry was standing beside their bed, her face flushed. When she saw Holly naked with a dildo, and Tori lying naked, Kerry covered her eyes and turned in a swift circle, before tripping over Holly's suitcase, falling head first over it and onto the floor.

She let out a yelp of pain as she landed with a sharp thud, which led Trudi to appear at the bedroom door, just as Holly turned to face her.

When she saw Trudi's eyes widen as her gaze travelled from Holly's face down the length of her body, Holly let out her own yell.

"Why is everyone in here all of a sudden?" Holly asked, her voice still sticky with lust.

Then she turned back to Tori, who'd moved up the bed in a bid to shield Holly.

When Holly turned around, the dildo and Tori's face collided with a sticky thump and Tori rocked backwards, clutching her face.

"Ow!"

"Oh my god, I'm so sorry sweetheart, are you okay?" Holly reached down and touched Tori's hair, before remembering she was still standing naked in a room, wearing a dildo, with two of her friends watching.

She turned back to Trudi, went to say something, but the words dried up in her throat. Instead, she did a 180-degree turn back to the bed, just as Tori sat up again, only to whack her in the face for a second time.

Oh my god, why did she keep doing that? What was wrong with her?

Trudi let out a yelp of laughter from her vantage point and clapped her hands, too.

"Shit, are you okay?" Holly asked Tori. She still couldn't quite believe what was happening and why everyone was here.

Tori, for her part, leaned back, clutching her face. "Will you stop doing that?" she said eventually.

"From where I'm standing, it looks like you've got a weapon of mass destruction," Trudi added, still laughing.

"Sorry!" Holly said, her mind cracked, her thoughts scattered. She wasn't sure how she was meant to react to this situation, but she bent down and grabbed a T-shirt, covering her nudity somewhat.

Beside them, Kerry clambered to her feet, rubbing her shoulder.

"Are you okay?" Tori asked through her fingers, still rubbing her cheek and nose. She'd pulled the bedding up around her to cover her nakedness, and she'd partially succeeded.

"I'll live," Kerry replied.

"I'm not sure I will after what just happened," Tori replied.

Holly's thought process was just clearing and she swore she was still seeing stars. Her orgasm was still fresh and pumping around her system, only now it had been gatecrashed by two of their friends. "This might be a silly question, but why did you just run into our room?"

Kerry looked at Holly, then glanced down, then back up. "Can you take that thing off? I can't have a conversation with you when you're standing with a green dildo bouncing between your legs."

Holly reached for the straps and when she looked up, Shauna and Melissa were standing next to Trudi in the doorway, both staring, eyes wide.

Holly sighed. "Can you all leave us in peace for a minute, please?" she said, as Tori shuffled forward and helped her with the straps. Within seconds, the dildo was on the floor and Holly grabbed her jeans and put them on, sans underwear. She didn't normally go commando, but underwear seemed a trivial detail right this second.

"I'm sorry to barge in at such an intimate moment, but that movement you may have just felt is a tremor," Kerry said. "An earthquake tremor — it's being reported on Twitter. So you might want to stop having sex and come into the lounge to listen to Melissa who knows a bit about this sort of thing."

"An earthquake?" Holly couldn't quite take this in. Hell, everything was wonky right now. But at least she was part-dressed and no longer wearing a dildo. She put a hand to her face: sex stopped by an earthquake.

This was certainly a first.

"Are you sure?" Tori asked, drawing her knees up to her chest.

"Yes, we're sure, it's an earthquake. So we're convening in the lounge if you want to come in."

"Or we could all just come in here and watch the show for nothing," Trudi added, grinning. She was still in the doorway, arms crossed, but Melissa and Shauna had listened to Holly's wishes and left. "I have to say, it was quite spectacular what you just put on. Pure comedy gold."

Tori glared at her. "Ha ha, very funny."

"A green dildo, though — I'm impressed. I would have thought you two were far too provincial." Trudi smiled, but then there was another rumble and it literally wiped the smile off her face.

The building shook just slightly: it felt like a truck passing by, only the picture on the wall fell off its hook, and on the bedside table, Holly's water sloshed over the edge of the glass.

"Shit the bed," Tori said. "That's really an earthquake?" Her voice was raised now. "I thought that happened like, once every 200 years? I checked before I came, I was sure that's what it said on Wikipedia."

"Yeah, well, blame global warming or something, but you might want to get some clothes on and get outside. I'll leave you to do that, I've seen enough already." Kerry walked towards the door, her face freaked.

"And Melissa is an earthquake expert?" Tori said.

Kerry turned, her arms outstretched. "Well, she's the only San Francisco native, so yes, that makes her one. She says it's probably nothing to worry about, but a lot of people in earthquakes die in bed because they're not prepared, so I just thought I'd warn you. And now I'm going. I'll shut the door on my way out." She turned and raised an eyebrow as she did.

Just then there was another rumble, and the fertility statue on the shelf above Tori's bed wobbled, and then wobbled some more.

Holly was still gathering her thoughts, processing the last five minutes, so all she saw next was Kerry leaping across the room, and flinging herself towards Tori, who was sitting on the bed. Holly's heart jumped into her mouth as she saw the statue falling towards Tori's head — but just before it struck her, Kerry's hand punched it out of its trajectory.

It was enough to alter its course, and the statue instead crash-landed on Tori's bedside table, smashing a glass of water in the process, glass skittling off the flat surface and onto the carpet as water dripped down the sides of the table. The statue itself skidded off the table, too, and landed with a thump on the carpet.

Holly just gaped at the scene, mouth open, while Kerry let out another yelp of pain as she landed on the same shoulder she'd just fallen on two minutes earlier. In saving Tori, she had also landed in her lap, pulling the covers down and exposing Tori's breasts, her right nostril now lying beside Tori's left nipple.

Tori gasped and rocked backwards, a look of sheer terror on her face.

"For fuck's sake, what's going on today?" She glanced

down at Kerry, then over at the bedside table, the shattered glass, the grounded statue. "Did you just save me from being killed by my statue?" she asked, eventually.

Kerry was still lying flat, getting her breath back. "I did," she muttered into the duvet, before rolling over and away from Tori. When she lifted up her right hand, it was bleeding. She flexed it and winced.

"Ow," Kerry said. "I can now reveal that punching a statue is not something I'd recommend."

She paused, taking the tissues that Holly was offering her to soak up the blood. She wound them round her knuckles like a boxer preparing for a fight, before sitting up, then standing. "But better my hand than your head."

"Oh my god," Holly said, rushing round to the side of the bed and hugging first Kerry, and then Tori. "You just saved her fucking life. That could have killed you!"

Tori still looked freaked. "It could have — I wasn't expecting an earthquake." She shook her head as she looked up at Kerry. "I don't know what to say apart from thanks." A dazed smile softened her features. "You really did just save my life."

Kerry shrugged, giving her a smile. "No problem — I better go and sort my hand out." She was clutching it with her other hand, pain etched all over her face. "I'll leave you red hot lovers to get dressed."

With that, she walked out of the room, and Holly could hear her explaining what had happened to Trudi in the lounge.

Holly turned to Tori, her emotions spilling out as she choked up. Her best friend had just saved her fiancée's life. Holly exhaled sharply, in a bid to stop the tears from falling. "I hate to tell you, but I'm not sure that statue is going to be lucky for us."

Tori shook her head, running a hand through her hair. "I think you might be right." She leaned over. "Mind your feet on the glass."

Holly nodded. "I know, I can see it." She stood up. "Let's get this cleared up and get out to the others, shall we?"

Chapter Twenty-Six

"There are actually around 400 earthquakes every year in San Francisco, but it's rare we get a bad one." Melissa was sitting on the sofa with a black coffee in her hand. "I've never had one where the pictures come off the walls, though, or where statues fall off shelves. That's new — but it still wasn't very big. Certainly not big enough to be reported."

"There was me, thinking we were just having some rocking sex," Holly said with a smirk.

"The earth did move, though, babe," Tori replied, smiling. Truth be told, her limbs were still weak, her body still recovering. "I can't believe they have that many earthquakes here."

Melissa shrugged. "It's just the area — we're susceptible. Everyone thinks the big one is coming soon, but who knows? My parents remember ones that were around seven on the Richter scale, but I've never felt anything bigger than this really. Doors might slam, water might splash, but nothing major."

"It was enough to freak me out," Kerry said, still

holding her injured hand which was now bandaged up, thanks to Melissa's first aid training. Today, Melissa was proving a handy addition to the flat.

"Come here," Melissa replied, pulling Kerry to her. "Don't worry, I'll protect you," she said, kissing the top of her head. "You deserve to be protected, seeing as you've already saved a life today."

"And the rest of us?" Trudi said, sitting cross-legged on a massive cushion.

"You're on your own," Melissa said with a smirk. "Run fast."

They all laughed at that. It was 11.30am and nobody had got much sleep, but it was one of those days where nobody was going anywhere, either. They all wanted to sit around and chat about the earthquake, even though, for locals, it wasn't that noteworthy.

However, for five English women, this was a story to take home and exaggerate. Tori was already pondering the mileage she could get out of this down the pub. And wait till her mum found out.

Or perhaps she shouldn't tell her mum: after all, earthquakes tended to freak mums out.

"Makes you think, though, doesn't it: life's short, you've got to live it while you can," Tori said. She'd thought of little else since she was nearly taken out by a fertility statue. One thing she knew: it was going in the bin tonight.

Kerry grinned at her. "You were certainly living life when the quake struck."

Tori smiled at Kerry: it was a weird feeling, looking at her and feeling thankful. "You know what I mean. But we are living, aren't we? I mean, we're doing the app," she said, pointing at Trudi and Shauna. "You're writing," she said to Melissa, "and you're travelling the world nursing," she said to Kerry. "That's impressive."

Kerry narrowed her eyes. "And where's the punch line?"

"Punch line?"

"Yeah, you just gave me a compliment; there's usually a punch line in there somewhere, too."

Tori laughed outwardly, even though inwardly she was cringing. Perhaps she was as much to blame for their relationship as Kerry, after all. "No punch line," she said. "I am impressed by you. You're seeing the world, being a free spirit. And you just saved my life in there, so I owe you."

Beside her, Holly cleared her throat. "What about me?"

Tori turned her head, squeezing Holly's thigh. "You? You're visiting your still-alive girlfriend, then you're going back to the UK to sign up for your new career."

And when she said it out loud, it was suddenly clear to Tori that was exactly what *was* going to happen. They'd had a few chats about what was coming next, but they'd never articulated a definite plan. Yet that had just dropped out of her mouth, and suddenly, Tori knew it sounded right.

"You're pursuing your dream, too," Tori added. "And that's perfect."

And she almost meant it. It *was* perfect for Holly, it just wasn't perfect for her current situation. But the only person who could change that was her. She and Holly needed to have *the talk* and they needed to have it soon: nearly getting flattened in an earthquake had pushed that into clear focus. Plus, getting a ring for Holly was now a matter of urgency, too.

Because if Tori did have to stay here longer, she needed to show Holly how much she meant to her.

And after today, Tori was crystal clear: Holly meant everything.

Chapter Twenty-Seven

Their time together had flown by, and just as Holly was getting used to being with Tori again, it was time to say goodbye. She wasn't ready for it and she didn't think Tori was either; they'd been skirting around future plans but so far, so inconclusive. She guessed Tori was going to stay in San Francisco till the end of June, but after that, who knew?

All of which had made Holly consider all her options — that maybe she would have to think about coming over here, seeing as she was the one without a steady job.

She wasn't completely averse to it, it just wasn't something that had been on her radar when she'd arrived. However, if the alternative meant being without Tori, she might have to *get* ready, and fast.

Tori had taken the afternoon off after a manic past few days at Babe Magnet and they were meeting for some clam chowder down near Pier 39.

Holly was late, having misjudged the amount of time a tram might take to journey down Market Street, the main road that seemed to run the length of the city. The answer was: a long time.

When she arrived 20 minutes later than scheduled, Tori was leaning against the railing, fiddling with something in her hands, watching the sea lions in the water below. Even second time around, Holly was still amazed how many there were — but just like before, their acrid smell made her nose wrinkle.

She strode across the promenade, looking over the water to the small island that housed Alcatraz, admiring the fog currently shielding the Golden Gate bridge to her left.

Holly shivered as she walked up behind Tori, deliberately quiet, grabbing her by the shoulders and kissing the side of her neck. Tori's skin was cold under her warm lips.

Unfortunately, as Holly's fingers gripped her fiancée's shoulders, Tori let out a startled shriek and jumped, losing her grip on whatever she was holding — perhaps some kind of jewellery box? — juggling it in an impromptu circus act.

The tiny box flew up out of Tori's fingers and as she lunged forward to grab it out of the air, she only succeeded in punching it further away. She let out a yelp as the box flew upwards, then spun as if performing a gymnastics routine.

Holly watched in horror as it then proceeded to somersault forward, before falling, almost in slow motion, towards the wooden platform below, bouncing off one sea lion, then another, before falling onto the wood beside them. The animals, for their part, weren't interested, ignoring the gift that had just landed in their territory.

Holly didn't think the same could be said for Tori.

"What just happened!?" Tori said eventually, staring, jumping from foot to foot and waving her arms around in an exaggerated manner. "We have to get that back." It was fair to say Tori was having a mild hissy fit.

If it was possible to have a *mild* hissy fit.

"Are you okay? What was it? Some kind of jewellery?"

All of the blood had drained from Tori's face, and she nodded. "Yes… it's some earrings I just bought," she said, eventually.

"You've been earring shopping this morning? I thought you were crazy-busy at work? How did you have time to go earring shopping?"

Holly's heart slumped in her chest. Tori had told her she couldn't take any time off work this week, and yet, here she was, going earring shopping.

Tori wouldn't stop staring down at the sea lions. "Impulse purchase on the way here," she replied, not looking at Holly. "Only, they weren't cheap. In fact, they were the opposite of cheap. And now they're down there with the sea lions. Sweet baby Jesus."

She leaned against the railings and exhaled a long breath, before standing up and casting her gaze around the shorefront. "I can't believe that just happened. How can

I have just dropped your… my earrings?" Tori stuttered. "How can they be in with the sea lions?"

"Is there anyone around here we can ask? Like a sea lion person?" Holly was craning her neck, but all she could see were tourists in branded trainers and baseball caps. Certainly nobody who looked like a sea lion tamer. "I'm so sorry babe, it was my fault, creeping up on you."

Tori went to say something, then shook her head. "It doesn't matter now, we just have to find someone who can retrieve the damn box. And preferably before one of the sea lions knocks it into the water." Tori's eyes went wide at the thought of that, as she turned back towards the animals.

"Please don't flip the box into the water," she said, casting a hopeful gaze towards the mammals below.

* * *

Of course, what Tori knew and Holly did not was that inside that box was Holly's engagement ring, and it was now sitting on the sea lion platform.

Tori was cursing herself internally — why had she thought it would be a good idea to propose down here in the first place? She should have just done it in a restaurant like most other people do. One knee, a red rose, moonlight, music. Suddenly, she saw the appeal of that — if you did it as the movies told you to, there was no way your ring would end up with the sea lions, now was there?

Tori exhaled a battered sigh. For now, she had to concentrate on getting the ring back and then somehow stopping Holly wanting to see it.

One issue at a time.

"Excuse me!"

Tori whipped her head around, to see Holly accosting a worker with a Pier 39 fleece on. She ran after him, and by the time Tori caught up, she'd just finished explaining the issue to him.

"So we were wondering if you could possibly retrieve the earrings?"

The man had a kind face and nodded instantly. "Where you guys from?"

"London," Holly said. "I'm visiting, she lives here."

The man gave a nod of his head. "I'd love to go there one day — it looks amazing. So for our British visitors, I'll do my best to get your earrings back. Just give me a minute and I'll go down and see."

"Thank you so much," Tori said, following the man as he made his way across to the sea lion platforms.

"Where is it again?" he asked, turning back to Tori.

Tori pointed at the sea lion platform with the small black box sitting atop it. "Just there — can you see the black box?"

The man followed where she was pointing, then nodded, taking the wooden stairs down to the platforms. "Give me a minute," he shouted.

"I really hope he gets there in time," Tori said. She

flicked her eyes to the box, then to the man. She wished he'd move faster, but she knew it was slippery and he had to take care.

Holly put an arm around her as they both leaned over the railings, watching the man's every move. "Piece of cake — he'll soon have your earrings back."

Tori ground her teeth together as time slowed and the black jewellery box seemed to fade in and out of focus.

The man edged along the platform, trying to move the sea lions one way, but they weren't budging. He looked back up at Holly and Tori, then shouted something they didn't hear.

Tori put a thumb up in his direction anyway — she had to encourage him, even if she had no idea what he was doing.

The man disappeared from view, before coming back a few long minutes later with a hose. His tactic: to shift the mammals by spraying them with water. What's more, the tactic seemed to be working, and Tori stood up taller.

Her heartbeat was slamming in her chest as the man sprayed three sea lions in a row and they all obligingly jumped into the water, all the time getting closer to the ring.

Perhaps this story was going to have a happy ending, after all.

"He's nearly there," Holly said, giving Tori a squeeze.

Tori nodded, too nervous to say anything in case she jinxed it. There was $600 worth of ring in that box, and when she thought about losing it, nausea bunched in her throat.

There was now only one sea lion between the man and the ring box.

Tori unclenched her muscles and relaxed a little as he turned his spray on the mammal — it was going to be okay.

A brief surge of relief spurted through her, as the final sea lion honked at the man, before beginning to slide off the platform into the water. The man turned and raised a thumb to Tori and Holly, and Holly broke into a spontaneous round of applause.

"Yes!" Holly said, as the sea lion moved its bulk left.

But then, with what looked like a theatrical flourish, the sea lion almost appeared to look up towards them, before flicking its flipper and knocking the black box into the water.

"No!" Tori shouted, her hands going to her face, her heart plummeting through her body as if she'd just been shot.

She crumpled in front of Holly, doubling up and letting out a wailing noise.

"Babe?" Holly said, putting her hand on Tori's back. "They were just earrings. I'll buy you some new ones, don't worry."

Tori shook her head, before straightening back up. When she eventually prised her hands from her face, she knew it'd be a mess, her mascara probably smeared like a drunken raccoon. She was shaking her head, not saying a word.

"What's wrong? You're scaring me," Holly added.

"It wasn't earrings in there," Tori managed to get out eventually. "It was an engagement ring for you. I bought it this morning and was going to surprise you."

She turned back towards the sea lions who were all now jumping back onto the platform, normal service resumed. "And now, it's at the bottom of the Bay somewhere." It was all too much for Tori and she put her head in her hands again.

"My engagement ring?!" Holly's tone had gone up a notch. "I didn't even know you were buying me one."

"Well that was kinda the point," Tori said, her face slumped. "And now… well, it kinda is a surprise, but for all the wrong reasons." She shook her head. "I hope this isn't a sign, the Fates trying to tell us something."

Holly gave her a look. "Stop going on about fate," she said. "I believe in it, but not for this. This was nobody's fault, it was an accident."

Her face softened. "And I love that you bought me a ring, I really do." She cupped Tori's tear-stained cheeks. "That's so sweet of you — you've got so much else going on, I wasn't expecting it."

"But you need a ring, too. I don't like being the only one engaged."

Holly smiled at that. "And you're not — we both are. It's just that you've got the diamonds to prove it."

"And you nearly did." Tori threw up her hands. "I can't believe it. Hundreds of dollars, down the drain."

Holly gave Tori a brief smile. "More down the Bay than down the drain."

Tori rolled her eyes at that.

Holly put her arms around her and pulled her close. "It doesn't matter, babe."

A few seconds later the marina man reached them, his face slumped, too. "I'm so sorry, I was so close."

Tori shook his offered hand, shaking her head. "Not your fault, but thanks for trying."

"No problem," the man said. "And look on the bright side: when they trawl the Bay in years to come, someone's going to find your earrings and view it as treasure." He smiled at them. "Have a good day."

Tori shook her head at Holly as she watched him leave. "He's got no idea," she said, before looking back over the railing. "You think we should jump in to try to retrieve it?"

Holly hugged her from behind. "No, I don't. I think you should let me buy you lunch, and then you can tell me all about the ring I nearly got."

Tori sighed. "You sure know how to depress me."

"No time for depression, I leave in a few days." She clapped her hands. "Come on, we're going to have clam chowder and talk about imaginary jewellery. Perhaps the next ring you buy me will be in the shape of a sea lion."

Chapter Twenty-Eight

The next day, Tori had a plan: she was going to get her arse into gear and show Holly *just* how much she meant to her. With her trip churning up such a torrent of emotions, Tori wanted to make it plain before she left, with no room for any misunderstandings.

After the Pier 39 debacle, she'd already put in a call to secure one part of her surprise for Holly: now it was a simple case of getting Kerry on-board to help her out.

She checked her watch: Kerry was running late. She'd just moved into a flat in Mission, not a million miles from them, so Tori supposed it was about time they buried the hatchet. After all, if it wasn't for Kerry, she might be dead by now.

Ten minutes later, Kerry arrived at the cafe, out of breath, her face flushed from the cold.

"Sorry," she said, eventually, ordering a coffee before unwinding her stripey scarf and sitting down. "My shift ran a little late, pesky patient issues."

Tori smiled. "It's fine."

Kerry relaxed her shoulders before continuing. "So what's all this about? You were very cloak-and-dagger in your text."

"It's about tomorrow and the basketball."

"Can't wait!" Kerry said, rubbing her hands together. "My first ever game!"

"For all of us. Only, I have something else and I just wanted to let you know beforehand, too." Tori paused. "I'm proposing to Holly at the game tomorrow." She waited for the response, but only got a quizzical look from Kerry.

"Aren't you already engaged?"

"Technically, yes. I wanted to get a ring for Holly, but unfortunately, I dropped it in the Bay and a sea lion disposed of it."

Kerry was trying really hard not to laugh. "I heard. That was… bad luck."

"You can laugh if you want to." Tori pursed her lips as she said it: *stupid damn sea lion*.

"Only because it's a bit funny," Kerry said, with a sympathetic smile. "But you lost the ring, and that's got to hurt."

Tori nodded. "It does." She paused. "I thought you'd be more gleeful about it."

Kerry raised an eyebrow. "You've always had a low opinion of me, and maybe it's partly deserved, but I think you sell me a bit short. Yes, we used to rub each other up the wrong way when we were younger, but times change."

She put her index finger to her chest. "I've changed." Her hand was still bruised and scarred from the other day.

"How's your hand?" Tori asked, wincing as she saw it.

Kerry held it up. "It's not brilliant for my new relationship, but it's a good job I'm versatile," she said, smiling. She sat back, assessing Tori. "Don't you agree, though, about us? I mean, aren't you a different person now? Haven't you changed since you were 20?"

Tori's mind raced through her life from then to now: university, Bristol, Amy, Nicola, Holly. Hell yes, she'd changed a whole lot, and none more so than over the past year.

She nodded. "Of course I have. It'd be pretty tragic if I hadn't."

"Exactly. So don't think I spend my time dreaming of ways to trip you up, because I really don't."

The barista turned up with Kerry's coffee, and she thanked her before continuing, sitting forward in her chair as if to give her words added emphasis.

"I'm one of Holly's best friends, and she's marrying the other one. Don't you think I'd want to get on with you? Holly loves you and that's good enough for me." She cleared her throat. "And I admire what you're doing, being out here, launching the app — it's exciting."

Tori folded her arms across her chest: then she thought that might be seen as too defensive, so she unfolded them and crossed her legs instead. If a body language expert had been watching, they'd have had a field day.

Old habits died hard.

"Thanks," she said, eventually. "You, too." But even she knew the words came out still laced with her old grudge.

"Now say it like you mean it," Kerry replied, smirking.

Tori laughed, shaking her head. "I'm sorry, I really did try that time." She paused. "It's just… we've always battled for some reason, so it's hard to shake my defensive nature when I talk to you." She paused. "And I know how stupid that sounds, believe me."

Kerry smiled. "So maybe we could shake on it — get on now, for Holly's sake?"

Tori nodded slowly. "Of course," she replied, holding out a hand. "Especially seeing as you're living here now and dating my friend."

"Thanks for that, by the way. Melissa is awesome."

"She is," Tori replied. "So, new start?"

Kerry shook her hand. "New start," she said. "Although not thinking about ways to rile you won't die easily."

"I'm well aware of that," Tori said, shaking her head. It was in her and Kerry's relationship DNA, so it was going to take some effort on both their parts. "You think this means we're grown-ups now?"

"Don't tell anyone, my reputation would be ruined," Kerry replied. "And seriously, thanks for introducing me to Melissa. She's someone I could seriously fall in love with."

"Really?"

Kerry nodded. "*Really*. She's amazing."

"Seems like I'm being a lesbian matchmaker in work *and* out."

"You're a natural," Kerry said, smiling.

"So anyway, tomorrow. I'm proposing to Holly at half-time, so I just need you to be onside, just in case anything goes wrong."

Kerry's mouth dropped open. "Wow, that's quite a feat. In front of how many people?"

"20,000, give or take the odd one."

"Brave."

"Or stupid."

Kerry grinned. "I was being nice seeing as we're friends now."

Tori grinned right back. "Yeah well, it's going to be scary, so if you could help keep Holly in her seat at the break, as well as giving me lots of encouragement, that would be brilliant."

"Consider it done." Kerry narrowed her eyes as she looked at Tori. "So you really love her, right?"

Tori nodded slowly. "I really do."

"I never saw it coming."

"That makes two of us."

"But just so you know, I am really happy for you both. And I can't wait to come back and watch you get married. And wait till you see the venue in the flesh — it's just perfect."

"And you're to thank for that, too. You're making a habit of saving the day, lately. Your reputation is almost in tatters."

"Don't worry, I'll leave here and trip up an old lady to get it back on track," Kerry said. "And who knows, now we're almost neighbours and with friends in common, *we* might even become friends. Stranger things have happened."

"So long as you have my back tomorrow, it's a start."

"Wait — did you get another ring already too, then?"

Tori grinned. "Something like that."

Chapter Twenty-Nine

"So how's it going with Holly there?" Tori's mum was sitting at her kitchen table, and Tori could hear the radio in the background, could see her mum's cookbooks on the shelves behind. Her mind wandered back to summer days baking in that kitchen, licking the wooden spoon, the smell of freshly baked vanilla sponge. Happiness seeped into Tori's bones, along with a touch of homesickness, too.

She smiled at her laptop screen before replying. "Quickly. It feels like she only just got here and she goes in two days. We're off to see the basketball tomorrow, and then that's it for over four months at least." She pouted. "I don't know what's worse — seeing her and then her going, or not seeing her at all. At least my emotions are steadier when I know I'm not going to see her."

Her mum snorted. "Don't be so ridiculous — that sounds like you don't want to feel anything, and that's not you. You wear your heart on your sleeve, you always have." Her mum scratched her cheek. "Have you spoken about what's going to happen next?"

Tori looked down, avoiding her mum's gaze.

"I'll take that as a no then."

Tori's shoulders heaved: she knew they should have sorted things by now. "We kinda have, and I think Holly's staying put. It's just a question of whether or not I do the same or if I should come home."

Her mum was silent for a few seconds before she spoke again. "Did I ever tell you about your dad and me, when we got together?"

"Probably." Tori knew most things about her parent's courtship, as they'd often recited stories to her throughout her life.

"I don't know if you do. About the job."

Tori's forehead knitted into an uncertain frown. "What job?"

"The one in Manchester."

"I don't think so."

Her mum shifted in her seat. "I think it was about six months into our relationship when he got offered another promotion. Quite a bit more money, more status, a car." She paused. "But it also meant we'd be living 200 miles apart and seeing each other every other weekend at best."

Tori shook her head. "No, you never told me," she said, warmth filling her up as she thought about her young parents, newly in love. "What happened?"

"Well, he mulled it over and I told him to go for it, even though I didn't want him to take it. Why would I? I loved him and I could see a future with him. But I also knew I couldn't stand in his way and I couldn't have him resent me." Her mum's face shone with love. "His family were all for him going, of course." She stopped, her eyes sliding upwards as she got lost in her thoughts.

"And? Did he go?" Tori needed to know — she never knew her parents had faced a similar dilemma.

Her mum smiled. "He was going up until the last minute, when he told me he loved me, and I burst into tears. He'd never told me before, you see, and now he was off. I couldn't fathom it. So I told him I loved him, too, and that was that. He phoned the company and said he wasn't coming, and he stayed where he was. And he always told me it was the best decision he'd ever made in his life, choosing love over his work."

Tori sat, dumbfounded. Her dad had had a *Good Will Hunting* moment: he'd had to go see about a girl.

"And how come you've never told me this story before?"

Her mum shook her head slowly. "I don't know, love — it just never came up. But the thing is, and what you have to remember, is that jobs come and go, and you can always find another. But love? Sometimes that only comes along once in a lifetime, and when it does, you need to hang on to it with both hands. Because it doesn't wait, believe me. If your dad had taken that job, you might not be here. Your life changes on these decisions, everything can change in an instant. So think about it is all I'm saying."

Her mum leaned forward. “And ask yourself: in ten year’s time, when you look back, what will be more important? Your job, or Holly?”

And just like that, Tori’s future was decided.

It was true what they said: mums always did know best.

Chapter Thirty

They got the train to Oakland for the game, and as they neared the stadium the streets turned into a sea of blue and gold. The Golden State Warriors were taking on their Californian rivals, the LA Clippers, and expectation fluttered in the air, as the noise steadily grew.

Holly had been beyond excited when Tori had produced the tickets for the game: having it fall on Valentine's Day was quite the touch, even Tori had to admit. However, now she'd planned the half-time activities, it had taken on even greater significance.

They strode up the stairs of the Oracle Arena, one of the final seasons to be played here if the owners got their way and moved the team back to San Francisco. But Tori loved this space already: giant scoreboard over the court, screens all around, and swathes of yellow seating waiting to be filled.

And today, it was about to go down in the history of their relationship.

Tori's stomach rumbled as she smelt hot dogs, and she

turned to Holly, just as Kerry tapped her fiancée on the shoulder, her hand firmly clasped around Melissa.

"Happy Valentine's Day!" Kerry said, giving Holly a hug. "I've got a feeling this one's going to be the best one yet!"

Holly gave Tori a look as she hugged Melissa hello, too, before turning her stare back on Kerry. "You feeling okay? Getting all romantic over there, lover girl?" Holly said.

Kerry simply shrugged, taking Melissa's hand in hers and kissing it. "You know what, maybe since meeting Melissa, I do get the whole romance angle. And is that such a bad thing?"

"Not at all," Tori said. "Even Holly's coming round to Valentine's Day with my powers of persuasion, especially when it involves beer and hot dogs, am I right?"

Holly nodded. "Totally."

"Shall we get some then?"

"Hell, yes," Holly replied. "I want the full-on basketball experience. I want to eat unhealthy food, drink far too much beer and be on the kiss-cam. That's what I've been promised and that's what I want."

"Your wish is my command," Tori said, knowing Holly's dreams *were* all going to come true, whether she meant them or not.

"Here's your ticket, by the way. And remember, sit in your seat, not Kerry's or Melissa's. The ushers will check, so just make sure."

She knew it sounded odd, but she had to say it, get it planted in Holly's head. She didn't want to make a big deal of it later when she might suss out what was going on.

"Since when?" Holly asked, taking the ticket.

"Since now," Tori replied. "Just sit in this seat, okay?"

"Seat 149, no problem. If Kerry tries to muscle in, I'll slap her."

"I won't let her, don't worry," Melissa assured her.

Chapter Thirty-One

An hour later, the four of them were caught up in the action as the players bounced and pivoted on the court in front of them, the crowd bellowing all around.

Having played netball to an extremely poor standard, Tori was nothing but impressed at their stamina and shooting abilities.

"There's never a dull moment, is there?" Kerry said, leaning across to Holly.

"The Premier League could definitely learn something," Holly replied, laughing. "I've sat through way too many football games that could do with a kiss-cam, cheerleaders and free T-shirts being chucked into the crowd."

Just at that moment, one of the Warriors scored a basket from far out, and the crowd went wild as the player high-fived his team-mates. Tori grinned, swept up in the atmosphere. She might not understand all the rules fully, but she understood that Americans certainly knew how to entertain.

Beside her, Holly turned and gave her a sloppy kiss: she tasted of beer and nachos, which wasn't a surprise given what they'd been ingesting. The tips of Tori's fingers were yellow from the nacho chips, but she'd only had a single beer so her mind would be clear for the big moment coming up at half-time.

Tori flicked her gaze to the scoreboard to check the time: two minutes to go. She swallowed hard and saw Kerry nod her way.

She was beginning to sweat, the hairs on her arms standing up in anticipation, her heart-rate beginning to thump in her chest like a kick drum.

The quarter ended and the half-time music started: this was her cue to ready herself, and ready the ring. Any minute, the spotlight would be on them. She gulped down some saliva, along with her fear and reached for Holly's hand.

Only, her hand ran slap into Holly's leg, because Holly was standing up.

What the hell was she doing?

Tori poked her leg, then tugged on her hand. "Hey, sit down," she said, with as much cool as she could muster.

"I need the loo," Holly said, turning to her, pulling her hand from Tori's. "Be back in a sec."

Tori went to say something, but the words got stuck in her throat. She sent a desperate look to Kerry, whose eyebrows were higher than she'd ever seen them before.

In a second, Kerry was on her feet, blocking Holly's path. "I wouldn't go just yet — I heard those women behind say there were big queues," she said, indicating with her thumb like she was hitching a ride. "Leave it for a bit. Melissa always does, don't you?"

Melissa looked up, just putting a big dollop of candyfloss into her mouth (or "cotton candy" as she'd told Tori earlier). She closed her mouth, but nodded enthusiastically, making affirmative noises. Eventually she spoke.

"The lines are always horrible right now. Give it five minutes."

Holly looked to Kerry, then back to Tori, shrugged her shoulders and sat down. "If the locals say so."

Tori let go of a breath she'd been holding for what seemed like five minutes, just as the stadium announcer took to the mic.

"And now we have a very special kiss-cam moment for one special lady in the crowd on Valentine's Day," he said, as the camera swung around the crowd, before it landed on Tori and Holly.

Holly wasn't looking, but Melissa was, caught on camera with a mouthful of candyfloss.

She quickly ducked out of view.

"Holly Davis, Tori Hammond has something she wants to ask you," boomed the announcer in a voice so deliciously American, it might as well have been wrapped in a bun and slathered in mustard. "Take it away, Tori," the announcer added.

The camera zoomed in, and Holly's eyes widened to the size of spaceships. "What's going on?" she asked, her gaze darting around the arena before landing back on the big screen. "Why are we up there?" she asked, pointing.

Tori stood in front of her, keeping a hand on Holly's shoulder to stop her standing — she could see her fiancée was going to from her body language. She still hadn't twigged.

"What's going on is this," Tori said, fishing in her jacket for the ring box. Her heartbeat was so high, she was worried it might soar out of the stadium, but her voice was coming out crystal clear as she got down on one knee, readying herself to propose.

"Oh my god," Holly uttered, seemingly not knowing where to look: at Tori or at the big screen. Her head kept bobbing one way, and then the other, as if she was watching a tennis match in slow-motion. "I thought you lost the ring?"

All around them, the crowd began to clap and cheer, and a wave of romance swept around the stadium like a sonic boom of love, making Tori tingle all over. She hoped Holly was feeling it, too.

When she'd come up with this idea, she'd thought proposing in front of a full stadium of people would make it more nerve-wracking. Never once had she stopped to consider she might be *spurred on* by the crowd, helped over the line by their momentum.

Right now, as her heart rocked in her chest and every hair on her body stood to attention, their swell of support was making this one of the most special moments of her life.

And sitting right in front of her was the one who counted most: her gorgeous, delectable Holly.

"I did lose the ring, as you know," Tori said, flipping open the box. "But I decided that the proposal could carry on, and why not make it as big as it could possibly be?" Tori broke into a wide grin as she fixed Holly with her eyes and held up the ring, made of sugar and food colourings.

"You got me a Haribo ring?" Holly said, beginning to laugh gently.

"I did," Tori replied, grinning. "I thought it covered all bases — you can wear it, and then you can eat it. When you think about it, it's way better than my first choice. Who wants a diamond ring anyway?"

"Not me," Holly said, shaking her head.

"Anyway, back to the proposal," Tori said, before pausing and taking a deep breath. Her blood was roaring so hard in her ears, it sounded like she was on a motorway, but she ignored it.

"Holly Davis, love of my life, now it's my turn. Will you marry me?" And now that the words were all out, Tori grinned for all she was worth: damn, that felt good.

Because when she thought about it, how lucky were they? She'd experienced being asked, and now here she was, the askee on her knee. And both times, she'd wanted to weep with happiness, thanking her lucky stars they'd found each other at last.

And when she looked into Holly's eyes, she knew Holly felt the same as she nodded her head.

"Of course I'll marry you," she replied, almost choking on her words.

Tori stood up, helping Holly to her feet with her outstretched hands and slipped the ring on her finger: it fitted perfectly as she'd known it would, seeing it was made of sugar and gelatine and therefore expanded to size.

Holly looked down and twisted it around on her finger as the crowd around them roared their approval, while behind them Kerry and Melissa were clapping for all they were worth.

"For once in my life, I'm stumped," Holly said, shaking her head. "I literally have no idea what to say."

Tori shrugged. "Then don't say anything, let me." Then she turned into the cameras, holding her hands aloft like she'd just won the biggest race of her life. Which, in a way, she had.

"She said yes!" she shouted to nobody and everybody, taking hold of Holly's left hand and holding it up with her right. "We're getting married!" And then, Tori turned to kiss Holly, searching for her mouth, the place where she belonged.

Home.

As their lips connected, it felt like 20,000 people

erupted as one — while inside Tori, her heart did a samba of celebration.

Sure, she'd already agreed to be Holly's wife, but now Holly had agreed to be hers too, the deal was well and truly sealed. If Tori had been a bit distracted with work of late, she hoped this went some way to showing Holly she was totally serious when it came to them. Because, when all was said and done, the two of them were all that mattered.

Tori pulled back and cupped Holly's face, as her partner's face crumpled into a puddle of emotion.

"Well you've well and truly trumped me — how am I ever going to improve on this Valentine's Day?"

Tori laughed a throaty laugh. "You can't. I'm the winner." She held her arms aloft again, before circling them around Holly. "Admit it, Davis, I'm the winner at romance."

The skin around Holly's eyes crinkled as she laughed. "You are the queen of love," she replied. "Here I was thinking we were already engaged, so this was the last thing I was expecting. Especially after you fed my ring to the sea lions."

The whistles and cheers from the crowd still reverberated around them, but the camera had pulled away now.

"Exactly why I did it — I knew you wouldn't be expecting it. The sea lion thing was all part of the plan." Tori cleared her throat as she laughed at her own joke.

"Plus, I wanted to ask you to marry me, too, and why not do it in front of all these people? No way you can back out, now." Tori leaned in and gave her another quick peck on the lips.

And then Kerry's hands were around Holly's neck, giving her a hug from behind. "Congrats, you two. And thank goodness you didn't go to the loo just then, or I might have had to accept Tori's proposal, and that would have been *really* awkward."

Holly smiled. "I did wonder why you were all so hell-bent on me staying put, but now I know."

"Congratulations Tori and Holly!" said the announcer, focusing in on them again. "She said yes! Good job!"

Tori blushed the colour of beetroot as the camera zoomed back in on them. "Okay, they can go away now, enough already."

"Time to act American," Holly said with a grin as she put an arm around Tori and they waved as the stadium cheered again.

Eventually the camera panned away, and Tori accepted the congrats of several people around them. She'd wondered about the reaction to two women getting engaged in a sports stadium, but she'd assumed California was one of the safest states to do it, and she'd been right.

Adrenaline pulsed through her as Holly glanced down at her Haribo-covered finger.

"I will get you a real one, I promise." Tori kissed her again. "Just give me a few months to save up."

Holly smiled down at her. "I don't care about the ring," she said, sweeping her arm around the stadium. "This was amazing — better than any ring ever could be. This is something I'll remember for the rest of my life, something I'll tell our grandchildren."

Tori nodded, a soft smile on her face. "Remember this when you're back in London without me."

"I will," Holly replied, giving her another kiss. "And honestly, how did you arrange all of this? It's like we're in a Hollywood movie."

Tori shrugged, coming over bashful. "It was one of the investors, actually. She knows the owners, and she told me when we were chatting that she arranged it for one of her friends. So I thought I'd see if she could do the same for us, and she did." She paused. "It was just right place, right time."

Holly stared into her eyes, shaking her head from side to side. "We haven't always been in the right place, right time, have we?"

Now it was Tori's turn to shake her head, as her gaze dropped to Holly's mouth, then back up to her face. "But we are now," she replied, closing the gap between them.

As her lips caressed Holly's, whispering stories of times past and times to come, a rush of love rumbled through Tori, slipping from her scalp down to her toes. She felt more anchored than ever, Holly's breasts against her, their lips pressed together, their hearts beating as one.

When she opened her eyes and drew back, Kerry was

giving her a look, and then miming sticking two fingers down her throat.

Tori, in reply, stuck out her tongue. "You're so mature, did anyone ever tell you that?"

"Says the woman standing with her tongue out."

"Suck it up, buttercup," Tori replied. "You don't get engaged every day, do you?"

Kerry shook her head. "No, with you two it's every other month. Are we doing this again over Skype when you get back to England or is that it, now? Are two engagements enough?"

Holly turned and put an arm around her friend as Melissa popped her head over Kerry's shoulder.

"I hope you know what you're letting yourself in for?" Holly said to Melissa. "As you can see, my friend here is a hopeless romantic."

Melissa grinned at that. "It's all show. She's a pussycat, really." She paused. "Now, shall I go and get us celebratory beers to watch the rest of the game with?"

"That would be lovely, thank you," Tori said, smiling at her new friend who fitted in perfectly in this new foursome, as did Kerry, much to Tori's surprise.

And then a wave of sadness hit her as she remembered this was Holly's last day, and she was leaving tomorrow. She cleared her throat, as if trying to dislodge that fact.

She wasn't going to dwell on the negatives on her last night with her fiancée, because this afternoon was a day for positives.

"You okay?" Holly asked, clearly seeing her face drop.

Tori nodded, watching as Kerry and Melissa climbed the steps of the stadium, Kerry laughing at something Melissa said. They were just doing normal couple things, the stuff Tori missed doing with Holly. The stuff she'd wiped out of her life, and now, she very much wanted to shoehorn back in.

The feeling of loss was starting to seep into her bones, and Holly wasn't even gone yet. She concentrated on blocking its path, while fixing her face into a firm picture of I-just-got-engaged happiness.

"Yep, I'm great," she said, taking Holly's hand. "I was just thinking, the timing of our proposals match. You asked me when I was leaving London the next day; now I've asked you when you're leaving tomorrow." She swiped her tongue along her top lip, then along the bottom. "You think we panic when the other is going?"

Holly put an arm around her and pulled her close. "Maybe a little," she replied. "I know it's crossed my mind already that I don't want to leave you."

"And I don't want you to go. I was just watching Kerry and Melissa laughing at something the other said, and they're just starting out together, who knows where that might lead? And I was thinking — we haven't been together long enough to be apart for so long — you're not boring enough to me yet."

Holly let out a bark of laughter. "I think there was a compliment in there somewhere."

"There was," Tori said, now more sure than ever that the decision she'd made on the phone call to her mum was right. It didn't matter where she was, as long as she was with Holly. All this time she'd been thinking of her career, of what she should or shouldn't do for it, when it wasn't what was *really* important.

But when she thought about going home to London with Holly? It made sense. Wherever Holly was, was home, and Tori was fed up of them not being together. Her decision shouldn't be based on her job, that's where she'd been going wrong; it should be based on her heart. If it was good enough for her parents, it was good enough for them.

"I've made a decision," Tori said, squeezing her arm around Holly's waist.

Holly turned her head. "You have?"

Tori nodded, steeling herself to say the words.

"I'm coming home," she spluttered, finally. An avalanche of relief tumbled through her senses, and she had to grip the plastic back of her chair to steady herself.

Holly furrowed her brow. "You're coming home?"

"I am," Tori replied, a grin plastered on her face as she took both of Holly's hands in hers and they turned to face each other. "I don't want to live my life without you anymore, and proposing has made me see that more than ever. You're the one that I want, Holly Davis, and I'm not letting you go."

Holly bit her lip before replying. "What about the

job? Trudi? What will she say?" She scuffed her foot on the ground. "I was thinking about moving here, actually."

Tori laughed at that. "It wouldn't work, you want to be in the UK, I know that deep down. I've known it all along." She paused. "I'm not coming with you right away, but I'll tell Trudi soon and get home by the end of summer — I'll aim for June, but I'll have to chat with her and sort things out."

The teams were back out now, settling into their starting positions, their long limbs ready for action. But what was happening on the court wasn't high on Tori's list of priorities: she was more focused on what was happening in her heart, and she'd just made a monumental decision.

Holly kissed Tori again and sparks of happiness flew between their lips.

When she pulled back, Holly gazed at her. "If you're really coming home, I couldn't be more thrilled. But I don't want to stand in the way of you doing what you want — you'd end up hating me. So this decision has to be for you, not for me."

Tori smiled up at her, a relieved, floaty feeling wafting through her bones. This was the right decision: it was the one she'd been fighting against but it felt like the perfect next move. She'd been holding on far too tight, but now that she'd let go, euphoria was oozing from every pore.

"It's totally for me, for *us*, for my dad," Tori said.

"For your dad?" Holly replied, scrunching up her forehead.

Tori waved a dismissive hand. "I'll tell you later, it's a long story."

"You better," Holly said. "But right now, it's a win for love on Valentine's Day?"

Tori nodded. "I'd say it's a slam dunk."

* * *

A few hours later, Tori led Holly to her bench by the bridge — or *their* bench, as she'd insisted while Holly was here. They sat down, Holly trying to ignore the chill seeping into her as she didn't want to spoil the mood. Holly was high on love and life, and why shouldn't she be? Tori had proposed in one of the most romantic ways possible.

And Tori was coming home, too, which was the best news *ever* — and it meant Holly wouldn't have to move to San Francisco, after all.

For the first time since she got here, her muscles unclenched and she fully relaxed.

"So today was quite something, wasn't it?" Tori said, turning and taking Holly's hand in hers. They could only vaguely make out the Golden Gate bridge, but they could see the headlights from the stream of cars crossing it, half of them red, half of them a hazy yellow.

"It was," Holly replied. "And those photos Kerry got were priceless. The look on my face." Holly shook her head — she'd been the definition of shock.

"Well, that was part of her job — to capture the moment. And she did it perfectly."

"She did," Holly said. "I'm really glad you two are getting along now, by the way. It makes my life so much easier." That was the understatement of the century. "So about earlier, just to be clear — are you really moving back home?"

Tori nodded. "I am."

"And what did you mean when you said about your dad?"

Tori smiled, clearing her throat. "I spoke to mum yesterday on Skype, and she told me about a similar situation with her and dad, where he had to choose between a job far away or staying put with her."

Holly shivered in the evening gloom. "And what did he choose?"

"He chose Mum — and things turned out pretty well for him, didn't they?"

"Not so bad. They got an okay daughter," Holly said, leaning in for a quick kiss. "So I've got your mum to thank?"

Tori shook her head. "Not so much. I was coming round to the idea when I was getting maudlin about you going home, and then when she told me that… it just made sense. I love you more than I love my job — and with luck, I can keep both. And if I can't…" Tori shrugged. "I'll get another job. I'm good at what I do." She paused. "But I can't get another you, can I?"

Holly shook her head, grinning. *When she put it like that.* "I'm one of a kind."

"You are — you're my kind," Tori replied.

"I'm glad." Holly paused. "But like I said, no regrets? You're not going to turn around in six months and throw this back at me, saying I robbed you of this chance?"

Tori shook her head, a slow smile spreading across her face. "A couple of years ago, I might have. But now, whenever I do anything, whenever something happens, *you're* the person I want to tell, *you're* the person I want to share it with. Because you're my *one*. And if you're thousands of miles away, I can't. So in the end, I'm not giving up *anything* — I'm choosing us."

Holly scooted closer to Tori, putting an arm around her as they both looked up at the stars. "You think your dad's sitting on one of those stars, looking down on us right now, smiling at your wisdom?" Holly asked.

Tori turned to her like she was bonkers. "Nah," she said. "He'll be out the back fiddling with God's cars. Or perhaps the Devil's — whoever's got the hottest wheels."

Holly laughed. "Hot wheels? Got to be the Devil."

Chapter Thirty-Two

With Holly gone, the flat seemed empty, and the Holly-shaped space in her heart had opened up again. However, now she'd made a firm decision, Tori was ready to take life and live it. She was going to enjoy the next four months in San Francisco, while also looking forward to going home after that and beginning her new life with Holly as a married woman.

She'd said as much to Kerry and Melissa when she went out for dinner with them at the weekend — and who would have guessed that was a sentence that would come out of Tori's mouth? These days, life seemed to have a habit of surprising her.

The one thing she wasn't going to miss was living and working with her friends: she just hoped their relationship was strong enough to survive. Trudi was still being impossible at times, and living with her only exacerbated things. Sometimes, Tori glimpsed the real Trudi shining through, the one she knew and loved, but it wasn't often enough.

She opened the fridge, grabbing the spinach-and-ricotta pizza she'd bought earlier. Just then, Trudi and Shauna walked in, and their entrance was like a pebble being dropped in the middle of a lake, the ripples of tension scattering all around.

Tori could tell something was up. She peeled back the packaging on the pizza and grabbed an oven tray, inserting a smile onto her face.

"Hey guys, good day?" she asked. Tori had enjoyed that rare thing: a day off.

Shauna rolled her eyes behind Trudi's back.

"Oh you know, I just wish my other half would back me up with decisions."

"It was the wrong move!" Shauna said. "Do you want me to just say yes to everything? I wouldn't be a very good business partner if I did that, would I?"

"I'd just like some support, that's all," Trudi said, turning to Tori. "It's not too much to ask, is it? I want to put something to the backers and she says no. Maybe we should ask Tori." Trudi folded her arms across her chest like a petulant child.

"Or maybe you should stop acting up and making Tori feel uncomfortable." Shauna shot daggers at Trudi. "Tori's not going to be around forever, so eventually we're going to have to work things out alone, like adults."

Tori's mouth dropped open: she hadn't said anything yet about moving to either of her friends — she'd been waiting for the right time.

Which definitely wasn't now.

Tori put the oven on, then the pizza in. But when that was done, she was almost too scared to turn around.

"Tori's not leaving, she wouldn't do that, would you?" Trudi said. "We're having too much fun." She scratched her head. "Did you and Holly talk when she was here? She's only temping, surely she could come here for a bit?"

Tori's facial muscles tightened as her smile got wider and more awkward. She was fairly sure this wasn't the time she'd been waiting for, but she wasn't about to lie.

"About that," she said, leaning on the counter-top in the kitchen. "We did discuss it and I'm not staying, actually — I need to get home, what with the wedding and all. I can give you a while longer after June, but then maybe we can talk about me working from the UK, or I can hire someone to replace me."

Trudi threw her hands in the air and threw her head back all in one go. "Well that's just perfect. My wife hates me and my best friend is buggering off. Honestly, I don't know why I bother."

She turned to Shauna. "I pushed you to do this, and carried it from day one — some gratitude would be nice." Then she pointed at Tori. "And you — this is the break you were looking for. You could work for anyone now, so a bit of loyalty would be nice. But no — it's shit-on-Trudi day."

She walked over to the fridge, brushing by Tori, and pulled out a bottle of Pinot Grigio. Then she grabbed a glass and filled it, before taking a healthy slug.

"I thought we were on the same page, that this was a journey we were taking together," she spat at Tori.

Tori's insides were raging, but she wanted to keep this professional. This was a work issue, rather than a personal issue, after all.

"Look, I'm going to cut you some slack because you've had a hard day, but I've done nothing but work hard and support you. But this is a decision I've made for me, and it's the right one."

"Right for you, maybe."

"Don't be such a brat, Trudi," Shauna said, walking over to the kitchen.

"Don't tell me what to do," Trudi snapped back. "Am I the only one who cares about this business?"

"I care!" Shauna said. "And I care about Tori and you, too. But lately, you only care about yourself. You need to look in the mirror and try to find the Trudi we know and love, because she's been hiding lately — and I know Tori would back me up." She paused. "And we should wish Tori well — she's done a fabulous job and she's giving us plenty of notice, too."

"I dragged it out of her — she hadn't even told us!" Trudi spluttered.

"I was going to tell you this week," Tori said. "I was just waiting for the right time, which really wasn't now, but it's out of the bag."

She paused, before pointing a finger at Trudi. "And yes, I agree with Shauna — you need to take a step back and stop being such an idiot. And you need to let people help you, and stop taking credit for everything that happens. It's a team effort, and you need to remember that."

"And my team is deserting me!" Trudi cried.

"Oh, save it for the silver screen," Shauna said, grabbing a glass and pouring herself some wine, too.

"We've been working our arses off and frankly, you've been a bit of a bitch lately," Tori said.

Trudi drew in a breath, wounded. "A bitch?"

Tori exhaled. "Uh-huh."

So much for keeping this professional. "You know what, I'm going to give you two a bit of space, get out of your hair tonight. There's a pizza in the oven, have it for dinner. And we'll talk tomorrow — you're too wound up tonight."

Tori walked across the lounge and through to her bedroom.

"You're just walking out?" Trudi asked, her mouth dropping open.

Tori turned around, nodding. "I think it's best, before I say something I might regret. I'd like to keep our friendship if I can, it means something to me."

* * *

Tori had no idea what had happened today, but she left the flat shaking with rage. She needed to talk it through, but it was two in the morning in the UK — 6pm here — so she couldn't call Holly, damn it. She flicked through her phone as she took the elevator down to street level, then found herself texting Melissa. Two minutes later, she got a text back saying Melissa was still at work, but Kerry was home.

Tori hesitated, gripping her phone, looking down. Was the situation so urgent she had to call Kerry? Yes, they were friends now, but were they friends who called each other in times like these? Her fingers decided before her brain caught up, covering the keypad and firing off a text.

Fifteen minutes later, Kerry walked into the coffee shop on Valencia, ordered her coffee and sat down opposite Tori.

"What's up?" she said, leaning forward and touching Tori's arm. "You can tell Aunty Kerry."

Tori filled her in.

Kerry sat back in her chair and blew out her cheeks. "I can't say I'm that surprised. You're living and working together, that's a recipe for disaster."

"But Trudi's turning into someone I don't know."

Kerry took a deep breath. "She just needs someone to take her to task, and hopefully Shauna can do that — she seems level-headed. Apart from when she was giving me the come-on that first night."

"She wasn't, was she?" Tori put her hand to her face — somehow, she felt responsible.

Kerry laughed. "She was, but sharing's not my style. I'm more of an all-or-nothing kinda girl." She sat forward. "Anyway, once Shauna's told her a few home truths, just have a chat with her — an honest chat." She winced. "But don't bring up what I just told you: I don't want to look like a prude."

Tori shook her head. "I won't."

Kerry refocused. "Just remember — Trudi doesn't know how to think before she speaks. I've only met her a handful of times and even I can see that. Surely you do too, being an old friend?"

Tori nodded again: she did. "You're right."

"She doesn't mean the things she said, she's probably just under a lot of pressure. Remember, this is fairly new to everyone, and she's not going to handle every situation like a skilled manager."

Tori narrowed her eyes. "Since when did you become so Zen and 'go with the flow'?"

Kerry gave her a sweet smile — she was glowing, inside and out. "Since I spent enough of my life focusing on things I couldn't change. Go on enough yoga retreats in Thailand, and you soon chill the fuck out." Kerry rolled her shoulders.

"This isn't a picnic for Trudi either, but you just need to remind her that your friendship matters, along with the fact that your life does, too. She wants you to stay, so she's acting up. She'll calm down when she's had some time." She paused. "And anyway, can't you do this job from the UK?"

"I thought so at first, but I think having someone on the ground and in the same time zone is important, too. But I could start up a London office, which I think might be needed fairly soon — plus, I said I'd hire my replacement. It just feels like she's thrown all my hard work back in my face."

Tori sighed, but she could already feel the weight being lifted from her shoulders just by talking it through — and Kerry was proving to be a valuable outside perspective with no skin in the game. Whisper it, but Kerry was the perfect choice for this moment.

"Like I said, just talk to her when she's calmed down. I'm sure you'll find a different person, one who's contrite. She's under a lot of pressure and she'd probably just had a bad day. We've all had them."

Tori nodded. "You're right, I'll talk to her." She bit her bottom lip. "So how are things with Melissa? Going well?"

The radiance of Kerry's subsequent grin could have been used to power the Giants stadium, it was so wide. "Melissa is a gorgeous goddess sent from heaven. So yeah, things are going well." She paused. "She's never been to London, either, so you think we could squeeze her in as my plus one for the wedding?"

"Blimey, things must be going well," Tori replied. "And yes, I don't see why not. It'll be nice to have her there."

"You should get some invitations out soon."

"I know — Holly's told everyone by email, but she's sorting them out — we're having a call later when she's awake."

Tori shook her head. "I'll be glad to get home and get more of a handle on this wedding. It's so weird being here at such a crucial time. I was thrilled to be here at first, but now I just want to get back to Holly and start living my life with her. Is that sad?"

Kerry shook her head. "I believe it's called love, and you've got it bad," she said with a grin. "Then again, so have I. It must be contagious. We should put out a public health warning."

Tori couldn't contain the surprise seeping onto her face. "Love?" she said. "You weren't joking, then?"

Kerry shook her head. "I was not. Melissa is perfect, which means I'm forever in your debt. Isn't life cruel like that?"

"Life can be so wicked," Tori replied.

Chapter Thirty-Three

The following day at work was spent tip-toeing around each other. Tori went out for lunch to get a breather but they were all being extra-polite, Trudi giving Tori shy smiles throughout the day and Shauna buying her a coffee in the afternoon.

Around 4pm, Trudi's head popped up over her laptop, and she was chewing her bottom lip. Weirdly, there was no clanking from her stud crashing against her bottom teeth.

"Tori," she said, her voice a whisper.

This was the first time today she'd addressed her without a work question. Tori's heart sped up. "Yes?"

Trudi continued to chew her lip, and Tori cocked her head.

"Have you, um, taken your stud out?" Tori asked eventually. She was craning her neck to see, but she didn't quite believe it.

Trudi nodded, sticking her tongue out, suddenly emboldened. "I did — got fed up with it." She shrugged lightly. "Plus, it doesn't really fit the image of a grown-up business owner, does it?"

"But you loved it." Trudi had always been adamant her tongue stud set her apart.

She exhaled. "Times change," she said, before lowering her gaze. "People change." She stopped, before looking Tori in the eye. "But I hope friendships don't. Are you around later? To chat back at the flat?"

Tori hesitated: she didn't want another argument, she just wasn't in the mood.

Trudi held up her hands. "I promise I'll play nice."

Tori smiled, reassured. "Sure, I can be there."

"Cool. I've got to nip out, but I'll see you at home later, okay?"

* * *

When Tori got home, Trudi jumped up and took her coat, leading her to the sofa and plumping up the cushions.

Tori laughed as she sat down. "You're overdoing it a bit now."

"You think?" Shauna replied. "I'd say she's got weeks of grovelling to get you back onside."

"Weeks?" Trudi said, incredulity lacing her words. "How about a couple of days and a nice glass of champagne to start?"

"You're being contrite honey, remember?" Shauna said.

Trudi nodded. "Contrite, right." She stood up before swinging around. "Shall we take the drinks onto the balcony? You think it's warm enough?"

Shauna nodded, getting up herself. "We could try."

Tori and Shauna decamped to the balcony, overlooking the park. The sun was yet to set with the clocks having recently sprung forward, which meant the evenings were getting lighter. Tori welcomed them back like a long-lost friend.

Sure, she loved autumn, but winter was never her favourite. The promise of spring always brought the promise of fresh opportunities for her, and during this year especially, that was true. She'd moved to America and she was getting married: this year had been chock-full of change.

Trudi appeared with a bottle of Laurent Perrier and popped the cork, giving a cheer as it spun off into the air.

Shauna peered over the balcony. "I don't think it hit anyone," she confirmed, before straightening up. Shauna had got a haircut today, and Tori couldn't stop staring at it.

"Your hair looks amazing!" And it did. Shauna had *always* had long hair, but she'd had it chopped off and hipster-styled.

Shauna took off her cap and ruffled her new locks, her face painted bashful. "It looks okay, doesn't it?" she said. "I decided one of us should have short hair, so we tossed a coin and it was me."

"You did not," Tori said, laughing. "But times they are a-changing," she added, pointing first at Shauna, then at Trudi. "You've got an undercut, you've got rid of your tongue stud — it's time to ring in the new."

Trudi handed her a glass of bubbles, then cleared her throat. "Never a truer word spoken," she said. "So, I wanted to clear the air with you, to put things right. And to say sorry."

She looked into Tori's eyes, taking her free hand. "And I *am* sorry for how I acted and what I said. You're my best friend and I forgot that for a while." She paused. "I was just having a bad day — I don't know if you noticed."

"No, you kept it hidden really well," Tori snorted, as relief spread through her like a sunrise. She'd been stressed about this since it happened, but she was glad Trudi had taken the initiative and apologised.

"Yeah, well. Shauna had a word with me, made me stop and think about what I'd said. Honestly, we're just happy you've been here for the start. We couldn't have done it without you, could we?" Trudi said, looking at Shauna.

Shauna pushed her Giants cap down as she shook her head. "Hell, no. I've no idea when it comes to marketing and, thankfully, I still haven't," she said, laughing.

"But I want you to tell me again what you're doing."

Tori frowned at Trudi. "What do you mean?"

"Your plans, what you're doing." Trudi made expansive hand gestures as she spoke.

"My plans, right," Tori said, using her thumb to demonstrate her first point. "Well, I'll stay here as long as you need me after June, then I'll go home, and maybe we could discuss setting up a London office after that."

"And you'll hire a replacement here?"

"Of course, I was always going to do that. I won't leave you in the lurch."

"I know," Trudi said, before holding up her glass. "Well I think that sounds a great plan, and I completely understand it — you're getting married, you want to be with Holly. *I get it.* And hopefully, if things work out, we can carry on working together when you get back, too."

She clinked her glass to Tori and downed a huge gulp, before grinning at her. "And *that* is how I was supposed to react the other night: being a jerk to my best friend was *not* on the agenda, so apologies again."

Trudi pulled Tori into a hug, holding her glass of champagne over Tori's shoulder in her outstretched arm. "Do you forgive me for being such a twat?"

Tori hugged her right back. No matter what, Trudi would always be her friend, and she suspected they might get back to that when they didn't live together.

"You're right, you were a twat, but you're my twat," Tori said, before frowning. "Although not in *that way*, obviously," she added. "And yes, I forgive you. So long as I still have a job."

Trudi drew back and gave her a kiss on the cheek. "Course you still have a job, you pillock. I'm not going to sack you just for going back to England, am I? And so long as you're not going to sack me for being a shit friend, we're all good."

"I'll think about it," Tori replied.

"And we probably will need a set-up in London if the numbers keep going as they are, so it's perfect. You can get some bloggers going, get an office set up — you'll be busier than you are here."

"Impossible," Tori said, laughing. "Thanks for understanding, though — *eventually*."

Trudi blushed deep red under Tori's gaze, casting her eyes to the ground.

"I always knew the old Trudi was hiding in there somewhere." Tori paused. "I've loved creating this with you though, it's been quite the journey and we're only just starting." Tori paused. "Even though you did try to take the acclaim for my engagement." She nudged Trudi with her elbow.

"I apologised for that," Trudi replied, looking wounded.

"All I'm saying is, I expect a mammoth wedding gift from you. This big," Tori said, holding out her arms as wide as they'd go.

Trudi bowed in front of her. "Your wish is my command. You're going to be blown away."

"In a good way," Shauna added, giving Trudi a kiss on the cheek.

"But soon, you can go home and finally get to be Mrs Hammond-Davis," Trudi said. "Or will it be Davis-Hammond?"

Tori mimed being sick. "Neither — we're not double-barrelling, it's ridiculous."

"What about when you have kids? Whose name will they have?" Shauna asked.

"I'll cross that bridge when we come to it — we both will." An image of her holding two babies in her arms flitted across Tori's mind.

Twins? Really? Where the hell had that come from?

"You okay?" Trudi asked. "You look a little pale all of a sudden."

Tori shook herself. "I'm fine, just a funny turn," she said, styling it out. "And you are coming home for the wedding? For definite?"

Trudi nodded. "Wouldn't miss it for the world — it's your wedding after all, I'd never hear the end of it." She held up her glass again. "Here's to you and Holly and your future happiness. And here's to your wedding also being a free bar, seeing as we're flying all the way over from America for it."

Chapter Thirty-Four

Holly glanced up at the arrivals screen and gripped the single red rose between her fingers as she bounced gently on the balls of her feet. Tori's plane had landed and this time, finally, she was coming home for good. In less than an hour, their new life would be starting all over again after a six-month interruption, and Holly couldn't wait.

She glanced down at the rose as she waited, wondering if it was corny. But then she remembered this was for Tori, who was a hopeless romantic — she was bound to love it. And frankly, she'd have to, because today Holly was feeling corny, her body churning with emotions she couldn't quite pin down. She was a walking Hallmark card, liable at any moment to blurt out how she was feeling to complete strangers.

She concentrated on controlling her mouth and her emotions, and on not telling the elderly man next to her she was waiting for her fiancée, that she was getting married soon, that everything about this year had been strange but it was all suddenly coming into sharp focus. He could probably live without that.

But Holly couldn't.

And as she thought about everything coming in the next few months, she could only smile even harder. None of it would matter one bit without Tori — she could have all the dreams and ambitions in the world, but without Tori by her side, they didn't mean a thing.

With that thought pulsing through her blood, making her heart race that little bit faster, Holly clutched her rose a little bit too tight, and one of the thorns pierced the skin of her middle finger.

"Damn it," she said, as hot red blood spilled out of her finger, and she sucked it into her mouth.

But before she could start to feel too sorry for herself, a steady flow of travellers began streaming into the arrivals hall, some of them running into the arms of loved ones, some of them making their way to the exit alone.

Holly sucked her finger some more, the blood showing no sign of stopping — and when she looked back up, she spotted Tori. Her girlfriend was slightly bedraggled and pushing one more suitcase on her trolley than she'd left with in January, but it was definitely Tori, her hair flat to her head as it always was after flying.

Tori looked up and their eyes connected over the throng of bodies, as if by magic. They were two halves of a magnet, drawn to each other by some invisible force.

Holly was on the move then, rushing forwards to greet Tori, who wheeled her trolley to a gap in the crowd and then abandoned it as Holly offered her the rose, along with her lopsided grin.

Tori stopped dead, assessing the flower, her mouth curling into a delicious smile. "A rose? You bought me a rose?"

"I did," Holly said, holding up her finger. "And you better receive it with grace because it just attacked me." She sucked her finger again, the blood still pumping. "Why do finger cuts always bleed so much?"

"Have you turned into a romantic in my absence?" Tori asked, stroking Holly's arm.

"Take the flower," Holly said. "Plus, I'm bored of it, been carrying it since I left home."

"It's a well-travelled flower, then."

"Tori."

"Yes?"

"Take the fucking flower so I can kiss you, please."

Tori's face broke into a grin. "Now *that's* romantic. That's the Holly I know." She took the flower and opened out her arms.

Holly shook her head. "You're an awkward bugger, you know that, right?" Then she swooped in and picked Tori up off the ground, burying her head in her neck and kissing it lightly.

Finally, she pressed her lips to Tori's, and the world made sense again: four and a half months had definitely been too long.

"But you love me, right?" Tori asked as she came up for air.

Holly pulled back, her eyes shining with love. "I do love you," she replied. "God help me."

Tori got on tip-toes and kissed Holly again. "And thanks for the rose, by the way. It was romantic." She held it up. "It *is* romantic."

Holly laughed. "Whether it is or it isn't, you're carrying it home. It doesn't like me."

"I'm never going to let it go," Tori replied. "I'm going to name it Rebecca and it can be a friend for Petula."

"You're naming the rose?"

Tori nodded, as Holly grabbed her luggage trolley and they set off towards the trains. "Uh-huh. You have an issue with that?"

Holly shook her head. "No issue at all." She put an arm around her fiancée. "It's just, nobody's named anything in the past six months of my life, and I was just thinking, I've missed that." She leaned down and kissed Tori again. "I've missed you."

"That's good, because I'm back for good now." Tori looked over her shoulder. "You're not getting blood on my jacket, are you?"

"If I am, it's because of your rose. Bad Rebecca," Holly replied.

Chapter Thirty-Five

"What about Hammis?" Tori asked, her feet up on the sofa, eating some Walkers salt-and-vinegar crisps. She'd been mainlining them ever since her return — it was one of many things she'd missed in America.

Sitting on the other end of the sofa, Holly was watching the football. It was Super Sunday apparently, but judging by their kits, neither team on the pitch was Holly's team, Southampton. Still, that didn't seem to matter — Holly was happy watching football, full stop.

"Nope."

"Dammond?"

"No," Holly said, laughing gently. "You know, watching football when you weren't here was so much more peaceful." She glanced at Tori, giving her the smile she reserved just for her.

It made Tori woozy: she'd missed that smile.

"But it was far more boring, too, wasn't it? Admit it, you missed my background noise."

Holly put a finger to her chin, in mock consideration, before answering. "No, I think it was fine as it was."

"Liar," Tori said with a grin, kicking Holly in the leg.

"Ow, that's my bad leg!"

"It was a tap, you big baby," Tori replied, leaning over and rubbing Holly's leg at the same time. "Why are you being so dismissive anyway? I'm just offering up some name suggestions. I didn't think they were that bad. Davis and Hammond could easily be merged into Dammond."

Holly cocked her head. "But it's not your name or my name, and if I'm changing, I'd like it to be one or the other. Why can't we just keep our old names?"

"Because I'd like the same name as you. And I'd like our children, when they come along, to have the same name, too. When we get married, I want us all to share an identity, to be a family. It's important to me." For Tori, having the same name was all part of being a unit, being a family, which is why she wanted to decide on what name they should take.

Between that and her words, she now had Holly's attention.

"You're cute sometimes, and surprisingly old-fashioned. But that makes you even cuter." Holly put out her hand for some crisps and Tori placed some in her palm. "I hadn't thought about it, honestly, but maybe it makes sense if we're having kids."

"*If* we're having kids?" Tori's brow furrowed. "I didn't think that was an *if*."

"*When* we have kids," Holly replied. "It wasn't an *if*.

We're having them." She paused, before turning her head. "One each, right?"

Tori nodded. "But not at the same time. I'm not having a baby race."

"Me either," Holly replied through a mouthful of crisps. "So I guess it makes sense to have one name when you say it like that. Honestly? I'm not that attached to my name. And there are a lot more Davises in the world than there are Hammonds, so why don't we switch to yours?"

"Just like that?" Tori couldn't believe this discussion could be settled that easily.

Holly nodded. "I don't see why not. Relationships are all about compromise, aren't they? You cut short your time in San Francisco to be here on the sofa with me. I don't mind taking your name in marriage — it makes sense."

A warmth rushed through Tori as she contemplated what Holly had just said. "So we're definitely having kids and you're going to be Holly Hammond?" She paused, rolling the name around her mind. "It has quite a ring to it, doesn't it?"

Holly grinned. "It kinda does. It sounds like I should be a famous film star or something."

She flashed her hand in front of her face, before sucking in her cheeks and putting on a Hollywood movie trailer voice. "And now, coming down the red carpet, it's star of stage and screen, Holly Hammond!" Holly sat back, looking very pleased with herself. "Maybe I should have married you earlier and I would've been a movie star."

"It's never too late."

"I think the acting boat might have sailed, but I do quite like the sound of Holly Hammond." Holly swung her legs off the sofa and shuffled closer to Tori. "Do you like the sound of Holly Hammond?" She tilted her head and kissed Tori's neck, not waiting for an answer.

Tori gulped: she knew the look Holly was giving her. It was the one that made her clench inside. "I think she sounds divine," she said, as Holly's arms snaked around her waist. Goosebumps broke out all over Tori's body and she clutched the pad of paper she was holding that bit tighter.

When Holly pressed her lips onto hers, white hot sparks of lust sped through her body, fuelled by the thought of Holly taking her name. It really would mean so much — it would seal their marriage like nothing else, make them fused in a whole other way forever.

"I love the sound of Holly Hammond more than you could ever know," Tori said, between kisses. "And I can't wait to have babies with Holly Hammond, either."

Holly kissed her again, before drawing back, her eyes inky pools of longing. "I wish I could get you pregnant. More than you'll ever know." Her breaths were thick and they caught in her throat. They were breaths of want, and of regret at what she couldn't have.

"I already know, believe me," Tori replied.

Because she absolutely did. Up until she got with Holly, she'd never wanted kids.

Now, she'd give anything to be able to make love to Holly, conceive, and carry her baby — but it wasn't to be.

However, she could do the next best thing: she could love Holly and make love to her like it was the most important thing on the planet.

Which right now, it was.

Tori threw the pad of paper off her lap, kissing Holly's lips again, slipping her tongue into her mouth, a bubble of love inflating all around them.

"I was going to do the seating plan, but it can wait." Tori grabbed Holly's hand, getting to her feet and hauling Holly with her. Then she stripped off her top and bra in one swift move, loving the look on Holly's face as she watched, transfixed, as Tori's breasts bounced in front of her.

Tori gave her best come-to-bed eyes as she held out a hand, moving towards the bedroom. "Come on then Davis-soon-to-be-Hammond — show me what you've got." She snapped her fingers in Holly's direction.

"You've gone very Californian since living there," Holly said, planting a kiss on Tori's retreating back.

Tori turned her head. "You like it?"

Holly grinned. "What do you think?"

"You sure you don't mind missing the football?"

"Get in the bedroom, Mrs Hammond."

Tori didn't need telling twice. She almost skipped inside, before turning around, then tripping over the edge of the bed and toppling onto it with a giggle. She landed in a heap, and two seconds later, Holly was standing over her, one eyebrow raised, licking her lips.

"I've heard of throwing yourself at someone, but this is ridiculous," she said, smiling.

Tori crooked a finger and beckoned her closer.

Holly obliged, stopping when her face was inches from Tori's, her breath hot on her face.

Tori held up a single finger and trailed it along Holly's bottom lip, before sliding it into her mouth. "And now, I want you to take my jeans off and fuck me like Holly Hammond, Hollywood film star." Tori felt the warmth between her legs as she said it.

Holly's face creased into a smile as she sucked on Tori's finger, before she stood up straight, hauling a startled Tori with her. Then she guided her to the closed bedroom door and pressed her up against it.

The wood was cold on Tori's back, and then on her bum as Holly's hands worked swiftly, tugging down her jeans, then her underwear. Tori stepped out of them without a word, guided by Holly's steamy gaze. She could almost feel her wetness dripping down the inside of her leg. When Holly touched her there, Tori couldn't wait to see the look in her eyes.

The look that told Holly she was hers: all hers.

Holly's hands were all over her, a blur of skin on skin. Holly's top was off, and when their breasts connected, silky and smooth, Tori pressed into her, bliss pulsing beneath her skin.

Then Holly introduced her tongue, her teeth, travelling from Tori's eyelids to her stomach: she bent, nicked and sucked, and Tori swayed under her touch. This was the lover she was to keep for the rest of her life, and that made her smile.

When Holly's hands swooped over her breasts and down her stomach, Tori reached out and held onto the door handle. When Holly parted her legs, Tori couldn't press back hard enough.

Seconds later, Tori's mind went blank as Holly slipped her fingers through her hot, liquid centre. Tori's legs held firm as Holly began to fuck her slowly, her bum banging against the door, Holly's hand cradling the small of her back.

With every thrust, a wave of desire washed over her, again and again, and she dug her fingers into Holly's shoulders.

"Is this film star enough for you?" Holly whispered in her ear as she picked up her pace, pressing Tori into the door.

Tori couldn't speak, but simply nodded and groaned, as Holly hit the sweet spot that only she knew. She was drowning in an ocean of sweet, sticky lust.

"I can feel your heartbeat on my fingers," Holly whispered, her breathing ragged.

"I know," Tori said. And she did, because it was inside *her* body, inside her very core. "Don't you dare stop."

In response, Holly licked her earlobe; Tori tightened around Holly's fingers that little bit more.

She was so close.

Minutes later, with Tori's face flushed and her blood pumping hard, Holly's thumb pressed down on her clit.

It was a moment of perfection, a crossroads she couldn't retreat from.

As Holly circled and pressed, Tori ground down on her, too. And then, when she hit the heights and joy chicaned through her senses, Tori squeezed her eyes tight shut, before coming undone. Her orgasm ripped through her, and Tori clung to Holly as she overflowed, before slowing her lover's hand.

And then she knew what she wanted to do next: the same to Holly. So Tori reached down and grabbed Holly's hand, easing it out of her. She groaned as she did so: losing her lover's hand was always bittersweet.

Holly's face was a question mark. "I wasn't done yet," she said, frowning.

"I know," Tori replied, lifting Holly's hand to her mouth, her heart still racing, her blood still coursing through her veins. "And you're not done. We've only just started." And with that, Tori opened her mouth and sucked Holly's fingers one after the other, licking her juices off them, tasting herself.

"Now, get naked," Tori said, fixing Holly with her gaze, her clit still throbbing.

***

Holly wasn't about to argue with Tori — she'd seen that determined look before. And having Tori suck her fingers like that? She could already feel herself pulsing, and she knew she'd be slick with desire.

She stepped out of her jeans, with Tori's heated gaze following her every move; when she removed her pants, Tori spun her around and pressed her against the door.

"My turn," she said, bringing Holly's head down for a bruising kiss.

And then, with no ceremony, Tori's thigh was between Holly's legs, shifting them apart, thrusting. "Shall I get the dildo?" she asked, breathless.

Holly shook her head. "Just fuck me."

And so Tori did, sliding one finger into her lover, then two, then three. "You're so wet," she rasped, sucking hard on Holly's nipple.

Holly didn't reply.

Rather, she spread her legs, immersing herself in their sex, emotion rising in her, like a kettle coming to the boil. They were both thrusting and groaning now, lost in the moment, all inhibitions vanquished.

This moment was real, and raw. It was all about trust, about knowing your lover, and about loving them completely.

Minutes later, Holly threw her head back, ignoring the pain when it cracked against the door. But she didn't care, because she came with a groan and everything she'd ever wanted was right there, in that orgasm. As Tori loved her, her gaze boring into Holly, she knew she could never be happier than this: her lover inside her, desire coating her.

As Tori slid out of her, Holly groaned, her body inching forward, longing for Tori's return.

But then she came back, only this time, guiding Holly's fingers to her, too.

Tori matched Holly's stance, legs apart, gripping her shoulder. And then Tori's fingers began teasing Holly's clit, and she shuddered; when Holly did the same, Tori followed suit.

This time, they were taking the hill together.

They locked eyes, and gazed at each other, explosions of emotion roaming all over Holly's body, their fingers never stopping. And then they were rocking together, round and round, dancing out their love for each other.

"Just there," Holly panted, as Tori found her sweet spot, while rolling over her proud clit; she stayed there, moving up and down, gaining momentum.

Then Tori was back inside her, fucking her, and any remnants of rational thought Holly might have been holding left her head.

When Holly opened her eyes, Tori's gaze was burning into her; and then, in unison, their thumbs glided over each and they both groaned out loud.

Holly was the first to topple over the slippery edge, with Tori seconds behind her, their fingers greased and nimble. Holly's body slumped, but Tori pushed her back upright and didn't let up, making her come again in a rainbow of mind-altering lights and colours.

Holly couldn't tell you what day it was, what time it

was or what year it was: all she could muster was that she loved Tori, and that she couldn't stand for one more second.

Together, they stumbled to the bed and collapsed onto it, Holly groaning as her body hit the soft duvet. Within seconds, she was back inside Tori, bringing her to another climax, her lover's chest red, her cheeks flushed, her body pulsing.

When Tori reached down and stilled her hand, Holly withdrew gently, and they lay on the duvet, hand in sticky hand, a grin plastered on both their faces.

Holly's chest was heaving, her breath still fractured, but her spirits were soaring high into the clouds.

She squeezed Tori's hand and glanced left.

Tori's eyes were closed, her face content.

Holly concentrated on her breathing, regulating it, stilling it. Her heartbeat slowed in her ears and she clenched her fists. Then another wave of desire surfed through her and she was falling through the bed, gripping Tori, a smile creasing her face.

All that existed here was creamy, sweet love, and Holly was coated in it from head to toe.

Chapter Thirty-Six

Tori was sitting in her new office, staring out at the London skyline. It was still raining, less than three days to go till their wedding. She kept trying to find the reset button for this year's weather, but someone had hidden it. And now here they were, their wedding week upon them, and it wouldn't stop pouring, and the forecast was for more of the same, ad infinitum. It was at times like this she thought she might lose her sense of humour, but she was trying desperately to hold on.

At least they were getting married in the same place as their reception, so they wouldn't have to *get* anywhere in the rain. Plus, when all around the country the weather was causing havoc, with people getting flooded and losing their homes every day, having a slightly damp wedding day seemed a trivial detail.

Except, it was their one and *only* wedding day.

Still, she was thinking *positive.*

As Holly had told her this morning, they had each other and they had a full wine rack, and you couldn't ask for more than that. Tori smiled as she recalled it.

Damn, she loved that woman, and she was so pleased for Holly, who had started her new course and was loving it. She'd also begun a counselling course part-time on the side, so she could provide holistic intervention when she eventually qualified.

Holly and Sarah had already had meetings to discuss their future plans, with Sarah also enrolled in a counselling course. Tori was so proud of them both — not only for taking a new career direction, but for overcoming their differences and now being friends and future business partners. Whoever would have predicted that when Holly found out her dad was having an affair all those years ago? Certainly not Tori.

As for her, Babe Magnet was coming on a treat in London, and she'd set up in her new offices a fortnight earlier, with two staff and counting. Today, she was interviewing a bunch of new bloggers over Skype to see if they had what it took to work for the company: mainly, a non-corporate personality.

It was surprising how difficult that was to come by.

Her new assistant sat down on the desk beside her, pad in hand.

JC was definitely a type A personality, ready to work and rock the world with her greatness. And there was no doubt since Tori had hired her, they were getting more organised, more visibility on lesbian websites, more of everything, really.

Now she just had to figure out what the J and the C

stood for, because JC herself was being very vague on the subject.

"Morning Jasmine," Tori said, squinting up at JC.

"Nope," her colleague replied, shaking her head. "Do I look like a Jasmine?"

"I'm running out of Js," Tori replied. "You're not a Jane, Joanna or Julie, nor a Jackie or a Jen, so what the hell are you?"

JC tapped her pencil on her pad. "I'm a JC, ready to work. So are we having this meeting?"

Tori checked her watch. "Fifteen minutes, and yes, we will." She paused. "Are you the second coming?"

"Am I Jesus Christ?" JC rolled her eyes at Tori.

"Okay, okay," Tori replied, waving her hands. "What if I make you a tea? Will you tell me then?"

"Probably not," JC replied with a shake of the head. "But let me make you one to get over your lack of detective skills."

Tori watched her go and twirled round in her chair. She really should press Trudi harder — after all, JC had been her recommendation.

But apart from the rain and not knowing her assistant's real name, she had to admit life was going pretty well for her right now — she was still waiting for the catch. Her phone lit up, interrupting her thoughts: a text from Holly.

'Hey, we still meeting at lunch to finalise the flowers?'

Tori texted yes straight back. On top of that, she'd

also collected her suit from the hire shop today, and she couldn't be more excited.

Holly had got a bespoke suit made, but when Tori had spied one she liked in a hire shop, she'd decided to go with that. Her mum had baulked at not buying her outfit, but Tori had asked her how many times she'd worn her wedding dress after the day? That had shut her up.

Today was Thursday. On Saturday, she was getting married.

Chapter Thirty-Seven

Tori was lying in her hotel bed the night before the big day, out of breath, grinning up at the ceiling. She'd just come for the second time, and Holly was lying on top of her. If this was what being on the verge of getting married did for your sex life, they should do it every single week. Her orgasm had nearly sent her into a whole new orbit entirely.

"I can't wait to have sex with you when we're actually married," Tori said, as Holly rolled off her.

"Sure it'll be very different," Holly replied, a grin on her face as she glanced back at Tori. "Doesn't getting married mean we stop having sex?"

Tori cracked a smile at that. "Just try it," she replied. "Not on my watch."

They were silent for a few moments.

"I still can't believe Trudi bought us a honeymoon to Cuba, can you?" Trudi had promised Tori she'd be bowled over, and she'd been true to her word.

"Nope, that's really generous. It does mean you have to work for her for the rest of your natural born life though, you know that, right?" Holly gave her a grin. "So, you ready for tomorrow, then?"

Tori turned her head so she could see her fiancée. She nodded. "Never been more ready."

"It means you can't have sex with anyone else for the rest of your life."

"Where does it say that?" Tori said, in mock horror, before rolling on top of Holly and kissing her firmly, pinning her down with her lips and her heart. "If I only have to have sex with one person for the rest of my life, you'll do."

"You've got a way with words, you know."

"I know." Tori laughed and kissed her again. "Seriously, you ready to become Holly Hammond?"

Holly broke into a side-splitting grin. "I can't wait to be Holly Hammond." She gently eased Tori off her, getting up. "But the clock says nearly midnight and I should go, seeing as you're superstitious."

Tori pouted. Yes, it'd been her idea to wake up separately on their wedding day morning as tradition dictated, but she was doubting it now with the empty space beside her.

"Hey, this was your idea," Holly said, seeing Tori's face as she did up her robe.

"I know," she said. "So go, before I change my mind." She paused, turning onto her side and resting the side of her face in her palm. "Next time I see you, we'll be getting married."

Holly nodded, giving her a final kiss. “I know,” she said. “See you tomorrow.”

Chapter Thirty-Eight

"I still don't know why you're not wearing a dress. It's a bit odd, isn't it?"

Tori gave her Aunt Ellen a tight smile, thinking uncharitable thoughts. Her great aunt had just arrived and was now giving Tori a running commentary on the things that were different to what she referred to as a 'normal' wedding.

Tori's mum kept shooting her apologetic glances and was trying to steer the conversation onto safer topics, but Ellen was proving a stubborn audience.

"Tori rarely wears dresses, you know that. This is what she's more comfortable in," Tori's mum replied, gallantly stepping in. "But *your* dress looks lovely, Ellen. Is it new?"

Sometimes, Tori *really* loved her mum.

"It is, thank you!" Ellen replied. "Got it 40 per cent discount at Monsoon. Very happy with it." She smoothed down her floral fabric and smiled at Tori.

Tori gave her a tepid smile back.

"Now, will I take you downstairs and we'll see if we can find a cup of tea?" Tori's gran asked her sister.

Ellen, nodded: this was a plan she could truly get behind.

"We'll see you in a bit, then?" Gran said, steering her sister out the door while rolling her eyes.

When the door shut, Tori's mum gave a sigh. "Sorry about Ellen," she said. "She doesn't mean any harm."

Tori raised an eyebrow. "I know, but she needs an off switch sometimes. This whole day, there's not going to be a dress or a groom in sight, and the sooner she gets the gist of that, the better." Tori covered her mum's hand with hers. "But I'm not concentrating on that: it's my wedding day, and I'm concentrating on me."

A worried look flitted across Tori's face. "You think Holly's okay? I keep worrying she hasn't woken up yet, or that she needs help of some sort."

Her mum laughed. "She'll be fine — Holly is a big girl. Plus, she's got her mum and Sarah to help her out, and Elsie. Elsie will get her sorted even if nobody else does."

Tori smirked. "You're right there. She's so excited to be flower girl, bless her."

"As she should be to her favourite sister and sister-in-law." Her mum grinned. "It's odd to think you're going to have a three-year-old sister-in-law, isn't it?"

"She's the cutest sister-in-law I could wish for. Plus, she calls my future wife Lolly, and that's something I can never thank her enough for."

Tori was dressed in a white suit and grey shirt: they were reversing each other's colours today, Holly opting for the opposite combination. Tori tugged at her cuffs and when she looked up, her mum had a tear in her eye.

Tori walked over and put an arm around her. "Hey, what's the matter? I look away for a minute and you're bawling?" She squeezed her mum tight, and her mum breathed in sharply, before pulling back.

"I can't help it, love. It's just — it's your wedding day. My little baby is getting married, and I couldn't be happier for you. *Honestly*. And you know, I'm so honoured to be walking you down the aisle. But every time I think of it, I think of your dad. Because *he* should be here to walk you down the aisle, not me. He'd be so proud, he always was."

She pulled away from Tori, wafting her hands in front of her eyes in an effort to control the leakage. "And I know, I shouldn't be thinking that, but I am."

Tears welled in Tori's eyes now, too, as the words tumbled from her mum's mouth.

"Was he proud of me even when I poured red paint all over his precious car?"

Her mum let out a bark of laughter. "Even then," she replied, taking Tori's hand in hers.

"But he kinda had a say in me being here, didn't he?" Tori said. "I'm back because of *you*, because of *him*."

Her mum shook her head. "Nonsense. You were coming back anyway, I knew you would. You're here because this was the path you were meant to take — you and Holly, together."

Tori smiled. "That's true," she said. "But I know he's always with me, because he gave me the nudge I needed. So I know he's here," Tori said, putting a hand over her heart. "He's always here."

Tori hugged her mum then, as tight as she could. They'd always be a unit, just the two of them, but Tori was about to enter into another union today, one that would alter the rest of her life.

When her mum pulled back, she smiled at her daughter, before holding her at arm's length with both hands. "I wish you all the happiness in the world my darling, you know that. But just promise me this: enjoy today, and always put Holly first, no matter what. She's your life partner now, and you should always do that."

"I will," Tori replied, giving her mum a kiss on the cheek. "After all, I had great role models, didn't I?"

Chapter Thirty-Nine

Holly was standing at the front of the mill house and her palms were sweating, big time. Hell, even her ears were sweating. Her own wedding was bringing out the very worst in her body. She flexed her toes in her brand-new grey brogues before taking a deep breath.

Beside her, Kerry was standing in an unexpected navy blue clingy dress, replete with heels. In their long friendship, Holly had only ever seen Kerry in heels once.

"My wedding uniform," Kerry had told her earlier, as if that explained everything.

Kerry kept turning to wave to Melissa, who was sitting with friends six rows back. Holly could hear all the chatter behind her, but she didn't want to turn around, to see all those people here to watch her and Tori. She was already nervous enough without looking at the friends and family they'd gathered. If she could fool herself it was just going to be her and Tori in the room, she might stand a chance of not passing out with nerves.

Mind over matter.

Plus, she was pretty sure that as soon as she saw Tori, all other thoughts would evaporate.

"You've got the rings, right?" Kerry asked.

Holly's mouth dropped open and a cold blanket of fear coated her body. "You had the rings — you're the best woman, remember?" Hot bile worked its way up Holly's windpipe. She didn't want to have to ask the audience for a pretend ring: she wasn't in a 90s British rom-com.

Kerry nudged her with her elbow. "Relax, I'm kidding! It's a joke to make you loosen up."

As relief flooded every corner of her body, Holly deftly kicked Kerry in the shin.

Kerry staggered and bent over, rubbing her leg. "Ow, that really hurt!"

Holly grinned at her, loosening her shoulders. "Now you see, that really *did* make me loosen up. I feel much better now." She paused. "Lighter, somehow."

Kerry stood up, still wincing.

"Thanks, you're a mate."

For once, Kerry was silent.

Holly rubbed her hands together, nervous energy zapping all around her system. "Tori is not going to be happy with this rain when she's wearing a white suit."

Kerry nodded. "True. But most wedding photos are from the waist up, so I'm sure she'll be fine."

And then, the opening bars of Stevie Wonder's *For Once In My Life* floated through the speaker system, and Holly grabbed Kerry's arm to steady herself.

Just remember to breathe, Davis. This was it. After months of planning, worrying and waiting, *this was it.*

Behind her, Holly heard the congregation rise and cough as one.

Holly took her place in front of the celebrant, and as the energy in the room went up a level, the hairs on the back of her neck stood up, followed by every single one on her body.

She began to float away, like she was having some kind of out-of-body experience. She breathed in through her nose and out through her mouth in an effort to anchor herself, concentrating on being in the here and now. She studied the stone walls and tried to tune into the sound of rain on the concrete outside. It helped a bit.

After a few bars of the song, Holly smoothed down the front of her grey suit and risked a look back: and there was Tori, on the arms of her mum and gran, looking every bit the bride in her white trouser suit.

Seeing her, a slow grin spread across Holly's features and her heart went into overdrive: here comes the bride.

Scrap that, here comes *her* bride.

On seeing Tori, Holly's body relaxed and she flexed her shoulders.

As Tori gave her mum and gran a kiss each, Holly held out her hand and felt Tori's hand grip hers, cold and clammy. She smiled at her, and wanted to say so much, but her voice was wiry; she cleared her throat, but still struggled with the three words she managed to get out.

"You look incredible." And she did. Tori looked tailor-made for Holly, the ying to her yang, the storm to her calm.

For once in her life, just like the song said, Tori looked bashful. "So do you," she replied, squeezing Holly's hand.

Holly squeezed right back and hung on, like she'd never let her go.

And she had no intention of ever doing so.

For once in her life, she had someone who loved her for exactly who she was, and her heart swelled at the very thought.

* * *

There were words spoken, vows taken, Tori was sure of it.

But right now, standing in front of the photographer and 60 guests all pointing their cameras her way, Tori couldn't quite remember the words with utter clarity.

The edges were slightly blurred already; she was glad there would be a recording she could look back on to reassure herself it *had* actually happened.

But then she glanced down at her ring finger and saw the evidence shining back at her.

Yes, she was married to Holly, the love of her life.

She was pretty sure life didn't get much better than this.

They were still inside the mill house because of the pouring rain outside its walls.

The one thing Tori did recall was Holly's gaze on her during her vows.

How she'd watched her mouth saying the words, as if in a trance.

And then, when they were done and the celebrant had pronounced them married, the utter delight reflected in her wife's eyes as she leaned forward to kiss her, Holly's soft lips landing gently on hers and pressing down as if to claim her.

As she'd pulled away, Holly had whispered, "I love you."

Tori had just nodded, not able to get any words out — saying the vows had taken all her concentration.

But she hoped Holly knew, seeing as they'd just pledged themselves to each other for life.

Right at that moment, she couldn't have loved Holly Davis any more if she'd tried.

Or Holly Hammond as she was now.

"Tori! This way!"

Tori turned her head and smiled: she had no idea who'd asked, but she knew wedding protocol, and smiling for the cameras was definitely on the list.

Chapter Forty

The venue looked stunning, with crisp white tablecloths, white roses and grey candles to match Holly and Tori's colour scheme. The stone walls added grandeur, and even though daylight was fading, the rain had finally stopped and the light trickling in through the tall windows held a faint golden hue.

As Holly and Tori entered the room hand in hand, their guests got to their feet.

"Ladies and gentlemen, please put your hands together as we welcome the stars of the show: Tori and Holly!"

The crowd did as they were told, adding in some cheers and whistles of their own, and Holly kissed Tori's hand as they weaved their way through the sea of warmth and love.

When Holly walked past her colleague Ryan and his wife Eve, she gave him a wink.

Ahead was a round table just like everyone else's, filled with their nearest and dearest, including Trudi, Shauna, Kerry and Melissa. As they approached, the whistles from their table got louder.

"Make way, make way! Ladies with shiny rings!" Kerry said, pulling out a chair and slapping Holly on the back.

"Did you get lost taking those final photos?" Trudi asked.

"Or have a shag in the loo, like old times?" Kerry added.

"Perhaps bring along a certain green silicon friend of yours?" Trudi said with a flourish.

"All of the above, obviously," Tori replied, sitting down.

Holly sat down beside her, feeling like she was in an odd dream. She was sure it would all sink in soon, but what everyone had told her was right: weddings were surreal, especially your own.

Minutes later their starters were served and the waiter filled Holly's glass with white wine as she stared at her smoked salmon with horseradish, potato and capers.

Holly bit into it and couldn't taste a thing: it was as if her body was working overtime processing her emotions, so her taste buds had shut down. She could see the salmon was pink, but it tasted like air. Instead of flavour, nervous energy rattled round her body like a hurricane. She still had her speech to do, so she had to keep it contained until that was over.

"So how does it feel, being married?" Trudi asked, leaning over to Tori and kissing her cheek.

"Hey, my wife now," Holly said with a grin.

"She might be your wife, but she's my *work* wife," Trudi replied.

"I can't deny either," Tori said. "And honestly? It feels… nice to have this ring on my finger at last." Tori held up her ring finger, her grin wide. "The marriage bit is still a bit of a blur, but this is lovely — sitting down with family and friends and sharing the day. I might even settle down and enjoy it soon."

"A glass of wine might help," Melissa said, topping hers up.

"You might be right," Tori replied.

***

Holly got up, adjusting her collar and rolling her shoulders. When the applause died down, she unfolded her speech and cleared her throat.

"First of all, on behalf of my wife and I, I'd like to say thanks so much for coming," she said, before pausing.

Predictably, the room went wild, and Holly grinned, flashing Tori a wide beam. When the crowd had calmed enough, she went on.

"Today has been a long time coming for me and Tori, let me tell you. We first met at senior school, when we both had questionable fashion sense and hair choices — Tori's, I recall, was verging on a mullet, which she's always insisted was her mum's fault. But I've always had my suspicions she had something to do with it, too."

Laughter reverberated around the room and Holly caught Tori's cheeks turning red.

She smiled as she ploughed on.

"We became firm friends at school, and made our way through our A levels before going our separate ways to university: Tori went to Bristol and I stayed in London. But even though we took separate paths and different courses, we still kept in touch.

"A lot of people have asked us if anything did happen between us before we got together, and the honest answer is — no. Tori had her life and her girlfriends, and we were just friends: the best of friends.

"That is, until Tori moved into my spare room nearly four years ago and then I was reminded of how I felt. And it only took me another two years to tell her — I wanted to take things slowly, play the long game."

More laughter.

"But in the end, I didn't need to tell Tori: she came to her senses and realised the pot of gold right in front of her, and now here we are.

"And I won't stand here and tell you there haven't been ups and downs over the past two years, because I think most of you know there have. Not the least of which was me nearly getting killed, and then, just when I was recovered, Tori moved to San Francisco." Holly paused, glancing over at the table. "Thanks, Trudi."

"You're welcome!" Trudi replied, holding up her glass of wine.

"However, she couldn't shake me that easily — and luckily she didn't want to. Tori has now moved back to the UK, and that's the best news in the world."

"But what I learned when she was away is that I'm a bit of a wreck without her. I mean, I function, I survive, but I don't *live*. Because when stuff happens to me, Tori's the one I want to share it with. And without her in my life, the spark disappears, the colour goes, and everything's that little bit more drab."

Holly glanced at Tori, but she couldn't look for too long; her wife was staring back at her like she was a goddess.

"But I'm here to tell you, the colour's all switched back on now and Tori has crashed back into my life and our flat. Which of course means it's messy again, and the margarine's left out on the counter, and she can't find her keys just when she's leaving the flat." She risked a smile Tori's way at that one, and the crowd joined her.

"But I don't mind one bit. Because, like we said in the marriage vows, and like I've known since I met her, I always want Tori in my life — and I couldn't be happier to have her as my life partner, my love, my wife. Right now, our relationship is just at the start, we're just clay. I look forward to us both becoming master sculptors, moulding our relationship into exactly what we want it to be for the rest of our lives."

That got a big response from the crowd, and when Holly looked over at her mum, she could see she was crying. She understood — she was getting quite emotional herself. When she'd written the words this week, she'd choked up; now, saying them out loud to everyone, the only thing coursing through her veins was love.

Pure, thick, gooey love.

"So please join me and raise your glass to my gorgeously impossible better half, the one and only Tori." Holly walked over to Tori and kissed her lips, before raising her glass. "Happy wedding day, sweetheart!"

Chapter Forty-One

Tori blinked rapidly, in order to stop her from crying. *She was not going to cry.*

She'd made it through the ceremony without shedding a tear, and she hadn't cried when her gran had trodden on her foot during the photos, even though it *really* hurt.

But Holly getting up in front of everyone they knew and telling them how much she loved her?

Yeah, Tori was on the edge. But it was an edge she owned, and one she was about to shout from. Tori had told Holly she didn't want to do a speech, but now, she'd had a change of heart.

As Holly sat down, she gave Tori a questioning look, but Tori just smiled. Then, before she could stop herself, she was quieting the crowd down with a wave of her hand, and it worked.

Even if that hand was shaking.

"I wasn't going to do a speech — Holly and Trudi can attest to that. I was very definite that a speech was too much for me, it wasn't my domain," Tori said, waving a hand in front of her face to cool herself down.

She was suddenly feeling ultra-hot, and she reached down and took a slug of water before continuing. "However, being a bride gives me the right to change my mind, right?"

She got a couple of cheers for that, and her Uncle Tony shouted: "Too right! Start as you mean to go on!"

Tori turned and smiled at Holly. "But after what my gorgeous wife just said, I couldn't not say something in return." Tori paused, rolling the new terminology around her mouth. "You know, I quite liked saying that. Wife." She licked her lips. "It tastes delicious. Go figure."

More cheers.

"But I'd just like to echo Holly's sentiments right back at her. Where would I be without Holly in my life? I don't like to think." She shook her head rapidly as thoughts of their schooldays rattled through her head, and then thoughts of Nicola Sheen and how she'd so nearly blown it loomed large.

It didn't bear thinking about.

But she hadn't blown it, because she and Holly were meant to be together: that's just the way it was.

"I'm sure a lot of you know, but I'm the scatty one in this relationship. The basketcase. The one with the crazy ideas. Holly is the solid one: she gets things done and she thinks about things before she acts.

"Let's just say, she balances me out, and I'm grateful for her every single day. I mean, Holly asked me to marry her and in response, I buggered off to live halfway across the world." Tori shrugged her shoulders in an exaggerated fashion and the crowd laughed.

"Some people might have read something into that, but Holly didn't panic. And that's been the story of our friendship, our life together — because we were friends long before we were lovers.

"And during our friendship, Holly never let anything bad happen to me. Lord knows, there was plenty that could have — cover your ears, Mum and Gran — but Holly was always there to get me home and steer me right.

"And now she's my wife, I know that won't change a thing. And I'm learning, too. Years of Holly guiding me have made me see the better choices." Tori turned to face her wife.

"That's not to say that all my crazy ideas are behind me, because they're not, but at least you know you've had an effect. I don't always stick my hand in a socket these days — sometimes I check to see if the switch is on — which I'm sure you're grateful for."

Holly nodded, a smile plastered across her face. "You've no idea," she said.

"But now we're married, I know our love is just going to keep growing, and when we have children, Holly is going to guide them, too, and show them the right way. And I'll be there to throw in some variety." Tori's heart pulsed that little bit faster as she thought about their possible future: every scenario she conjured up was picture perfect.

"But seriously, Holly is so many things to me, but most of all, she's my best friend. And to be able to marry my best friend? Well, I think that makes me the luckiest woman alive."

Tori picked up her glass and kissed Holly on the lips. "Ladies and gentlemen, please raise your glasses to my one true love: it took us long enough to get here, but I look forward to a lifetime of discovery with you." She lifted her glass in the air. "To Holly, and to love."

"To Holly and to love!" The room chorused back.

Holly smiled up at her wife, shaking her head slowly. "You never fail to surprise me, you know."

"That's my evil plan," Tori replied.

Chapter Forty-Two

They'd avoided choosing their first dance song until the last minute, and they'd settled on the Dirty Dancing classic, 'The Time Of My Life'. However, when the DJ called them up to the dance floor, Holly wasn't ready at all.

"Whose idea was this? Why on earth did we choose such a classic dance number? We haven't even practised the lift!" she said, taking Tori's hand. Really, what had they been thinking?

"Just shut up and dance," Tori said with a grin, taking hold of Holly and doing just that. "You like dancing, remember?"

Holly glanced around the room at all their guests smiling at them. "Normally, yes." But right now, her feet felt like they were encased in lead.

However, Tori simply pulled her close and kissed her lips, which caused a cheer around the room.

And that was all it took for Holly to feel emboldened, so she kissed Tori right back, before spinning her out, then back again.

"Well in that case, let's give them a show," Holly said, straightening her shoulders and taking the lead.

She had this.

* * *

Half an hour later, the dance floor was filled, the DJ working her magic, playing the strict playlist Holly had given her. Every song she'd played so far, Holly had loved — sometimes, running the party had its perks.

And now, Holly was on the dance floor in the arms of her dad, letting him lead the way.

To her left, Tori was dancing with her cousin Todd, laughing at something he said. Meanwhile, next to them, Tori's gran was in the arms of a far younger man and looking extremely pleased about it; and to Holly's right, Melissa and Kerry were staring into each other's eyes, and Holly would lay bets they were wondering if this might be them one day, possibly sooner than anyone expected. She smiled at the thought.

"You planned a great day, you know," her dad said, smiling at her. "It's been different, but in a good way."

"A gay way?" Holly asked, laughing as they turned slowly.

But her dad shook his head. "In a *you* way. I wouldn't expect a normal wedding from you whether you were gay or straight, so it fitted perfectly."

"And you didn't mind not being able to give me away?" Holly had worried about that for a while, until she spoke to her dad beforehand and he'd assured her he was fine with it.

Again, he shook his head. "Not a bit — I'm still your dad, whether I walk you up the aisle or not." He paused, gripping Holly's hand that bit tighter. "Besides, you don't need giving away — you're old enough to look after yourself. Bit old-fashioned when you think about it, isn't it?"

Holly nodded. "Just a bit."

Her dad pursed his lips before speaking again. "And are you happy? You look happy." Her dad lowered his gaze as he asked her: talking about emotions didn't come naturally to him.

But Holly could do nothing but smile. "I'm beyond happy, so you don't have to worry about me. I've married my soulmate."

Her dad nodded. "You seem to have, and I'm chuffed for you. It's all you can hope for, as a parent."

The moment was interrupted by Elsie, tugging on Holly's cuff, her arms up in the air. "Lolly, pick me up!"

Holly laughed, doing as instructed and picking up her toddler sister, before bringing her back into their father–daughter embrace. "You want to dance, too?" Holly asked her.

Elsie nodded. "I've been dancing, but sometimes I like to dance up high." She paused. "Hello, Daddy," Elsie added, slapping the side of his head.

Their dad grinned. "Hello Elsie," he replied. "Are you enjoying Holly's wedding?"

Elsie nodded, her tiny face consumed by her smile. "I love it — there's cake!"

"There is," he agreed. "Do you think you might like to get married one day?"

Elsie considered it for a minute. "Would I get cake?"

"You get anything you want, you're the bride," Holly replied.

Elsie clapped her hands together. "Then I'm getting married to a lady, too!"

***

"So what do you think? Good day? Bad day? Indifferent day?" Holly was sitting next to Tori and it was 12.15am, no longer their wedding day. The lights were up, the crowd was dispersing and they had a rare minute to themselves.

Tori shrugged. "It was okay. Mediocre. I've had better." She could hardly contain her grin.

Holly nodded. "Like when there was a sale on at TK Maxx."

"That day was *the best*," Tori enthused.

"Or when you got a free side at Nando's?"

"Off the charts."

"But today? Your wedding day?"

Tori smiled at her, trailing a finger down Holly's cheek. Her wife looked tired, happy and beautiful.

To Tori, she was hands-down the most beautiful woman in the world.

"Honestly? It couldn't have been any better. Well, apart from the rain, but other than that..." She paused. "For starters, my wife was the best-looking woman in the room—"

"—no, mine was—"

"—we'll agree to differ," Tori said. "Plus, the food was surprisingly good and the drinks were free—"

"—about that," Holly interrupted, her index finger raised.

Tori waved a hand. "Tell me later." She paused. "But most of all, just gathering all of our family and friends together in this room, and feeling the explosion of love. I don't think I'll ever forget it."

And she wouldn't. Everyone said your wedding day was the best day of your life, and Tori had always called bullshit. But much to her surprise, hers *had* been. However, she knew that was down to her choice of mate, her one and only.

As the Americans would say, she'd married good.

"I'll never forget it, either," Holly said, planting a brief kiss on Tori's lips. "I'll never forget saying I do to you, or how gorgeous you looked walking down the aisle."

"Stop it," Tori said, blushing.

"But now it's over."

"It is for everyone else, but it's just the start for us," Tori said. "And we're starting it off right, with a honeymoon to Cuba."

"Thanks, Trudi!" Holly said, holding up her glass of red wine.

Tori clinked it with her own. "But first, we should help our parents get all this stuff together — cards, presents, all of that. I said I'd tell Mum where to put them, and then she said we could bugger off and do 'whatever it was we wanted to do'." Tori put the last part in finger quotes.

"Did she say those words?" Holly grinned.

"I'm quoting precisely," Tori said with a smile, before kissing her wife on the lips. "So shall we, then? Go tell Mum what to do, then you can carry me over the threshold of the bridal suite?"

Holly nodded, holding Tori's gaze. "Start as we mean to go on," she said, getting up and holding out her hand to Tori, who took it immediately. "Ready, Mrs Hammond?"

Tori laughed. "Born ready, Mrs Hammond," she replied.

Epilogue: Five Years Later

"Babe!" Tori shouted. At her raised voice, Valentine jumped off the sofa and ran out of the room, his ginger fur disappearing out the door in a blur.

Tori tutted. She couldn't run after him, not in her state.

"Valentine," she called softly. "Don't be such a wuss."

Tori was sitting in the lounge of their new home, rubbing her swollen ankles. Of all the side effects of pregnancy, nobody had warned her about swollen ankles — the days when her legs used to slim down between her calf and her foot were long gone; just like the days when she and Holly used to go out for dinner or a night out in the pub.

Being pregnant didn't have a lot of upsides, but the plus points were nearly here: she was due in just over a week, and she couldn't wait to meet her babies. For now, they had to get out of the house and get to Elsie's nativity to see her play Mary — they'd heard of nothing else for weeks and being late wasn't an option.

"Babe!" she shouted again. Where the hell was Holly? She swore she'd just gone upstairs to get her coat, and it wasn't like their new house was a mansion. Compared to their old central London flat, of course, it *was* a mansion, but still.

She was just about to shout again when she heard footsteps on the bare wooden stairs: the carpet fitters were due tomorrow to lay the new carpet on their hallway and stairs, just in time for their new arrivals.

"Where did you go?" Tori asked, heaving herself forwards, but waiting for a helping hand from Holly to get herself fully upright.

Holly knew her role and duly assisted, Tori groaning involuntarily as she stood.

"I had to nip to the loo," Holly said, rubbing her hands together. "It's bloody freezing in this house, my fingers are blue."

"It'll be better when there's carpet down, you know that."

Holly blew on her hands. "It better be," she said. "I don't want our new arrivals coming into a freezing house." She rubbed Tori's belly, as was her want. "They'll go into shock, seeing as they've been so lovely and warm inside you for the past nine months."

"Well, the quicker they get out, the better as far as I'm concerned. I'm over carrying two people around inside me now. Enough already." She waddled over to the sofa, then winced. "I think I might have to go to the loo again before we leave. Do you mind?"

Holly smiled, then held out her hand. "You're carrying our children, why would I mind?"

***

Holly kissed Tori's temple and gazed down at the two tiny humans; one resting on Tori's chest, the other in her arms.

Two healthy babies, and they were both theirs.

Even though she wasn't daunted exactly, the thought almost made her legs buckle. But that was soon wiped away when she kissed her daughter's head and breathed in her fresh baby smell. The doctors and nurses had all just left; now it was just the four of them.

Tori was lying in her hospital bed, her skin pale grey, but with the widest smile after giving birth. And after watching her do it, Holly was pretty sure Tori had the upper hand in every argument for the rest of their lives. Anyone who claimed women were the weaker sex had obviously never experienced what they just had.

To Tori's left, clinical white machines sat still, their job done. Someone had tried to introduce a little festive spirit by wrapping gold tinsel around the top, while the drip Tori was attached to had a Santa hat on. But none of that was as impressive as what was in their hands: their babies.

"They're just so… tiny, aren't they?" Tori said, her eyes never leaving the top of her son's head. "A boy and a girl: I couldn't dream of anything better, could you?"

Holly shook her head, kissing the top of her little girl's head. *Her daughter.* "Nope. The only thing more magnificent is you."

Tori smiled a tired smile. "I've never felt more tired or more happy. I want to dance, but I can't move." She looked up at Holly, then put out a hand to touch her daughter. "Will you call mum for me? You better tell everyone soon, or they'll be annoyed."

Holly smiled, kissing her daughter again. "They can wait."

And they could. She didn't want to leave this happy bubble of love she was luxuriating in, all warm and baby-scented. "Soon enough everyone will be all over us, but we can have five minutes together, can't we? Five minutes for me, you, Kanye and Kim."

Tori smiled, leaning her head back into her pillow. "We are not calling them Kanye and Kim."

"Spoilsport."

Tori kissed her son, then stroked the top of his head. Holly had only cut the umbilical cord less than 30 minutes ago, and the babies were both doing well, breathing on their own and adjusting to their first hour in the world.

"I was thinking — I know we had a ton of names we were considering, but do you think we could name him after dad? I know I thought that might be too sentimental, but he sort of looks like him."

"A bit wrinkled?" Holly said with a smile.

"Maybe that's it." Tori glanced up at Holly. "What do you think?"

Holly nodded. She'd always loved Tori's dad, and luckily he'd been called Richard and not anything hideous.

"You're right," she said. "He looks like a Richard to me, too." She kissed the top of his head. "Welcome to the world, Richard."

Two tears tracked their way down Tori's cheek as she kissed her son, too. "You're perfect, Richard. Just like your granddad."

Holly jiggled her daughter as she moved in her arms, her tiny head covered in a thick mop of dark hair. "What about this one?" she said. "Are we going for Charlotte?"

Tori nodded. "Richard and Charlotte: I like the sound of that. Charlie and Rich."

"Dickie and Charlie: they sound like a double act from the 1920s."

"Maybe they can open for their Auntie Elsie," Tori said.

Holly laughed gently. "Maybe." She paused. "This is it, though: this is us."

Tori glanced up at her, then back at her son. "Yep — we're four now, not two." Tori paused. "And you know what this means?"

"What?"

"That you might not have to get pregnant, after all."

"Damn," Holly said, with a smile. She'd always been scared of getting pregnant — and now she'd seen the birth, her fears hadn't lessened. But was she missing out on something if she didn't give birth herself? "I'm not ruling it out completely," she added.

"Really?"

"Let's see how difficult Dickie and Charlie are, first."

"Are you mad they were born on Christmas Day, too? Your birthday?"

Holly laughed again, shaking her head. "I'm thinking it means giant Christmases for us now for the rest of our lives."

"You'll get no complaints here," Tori said, her features softened with love. "Isn't it funny that all those years ago, when I was a young, stupid 27, all I wanted for Christmas was a girlfriend — and that girlfriend turned out to be you." Tori glanced up at Holly, kissing Richard's head again.

"And now look — we're married *and* we got two children for Christmas. I still can't quite believe it." Tori paused. "Can you?"

Holly shook her head. "No," she replied gently. "We're parents now. Actual *grown-up parents*. And our parents are grandparents."

"I know," Tori replied. "The circle of life." She reached out and touched Charlotte's arm. "Is she awake?"

Holly looked down at her daughter, both eyes tight shut. "Kinda. She does keep trying to open her eyes, but she just needs a little more practice.

"She's only 45 minutes old, give her time," Tori said, her smile now a permanent feature, lighting up the room.

"So what do you think?" Holly asked. "Have all your dreams come true?"

Tori nodded slowly. "They have. I've got you, and now

we've got these two," she said, glancing at her children. "I'm pretty lucky, aren't I?"

"We both are," Holly replied, a contented haze oozing softly through her. "And I suppose I should let the rest of the world in on our secret now, too."

She could already imagine the screams down the phone when she told her mum she was a grandma to a boy *and* a girl, never mind Tori's mum. Yep, these children were going to be spoilt rotten.

Holly looked around, taking a deep breath in. "I'm just soaking this up, the last time ever it's just going to be us four and nobody else involved." She put Charlotte down in a nearby cot: she didn't stir.

"I'm going to nip out to let the parents know." Holly grabbed her phone from her bag. "Is there anything you want?"

Tori smiled, before shaking her head. "Nope," she said. "Everything I want is right here."

THE END

Want more from me? Sign up to join my VIP Readers' Group and get a FREE lesbian romance,
It Had To Be You! *Claim your free book here:*
www.clarelydon.co.uk/it-had-to-be-you

Did You Enjoy This Book?

If the answer's yes, I wonder if you'd consider leaving me a review wherever you bought it. Just a line or two is fine, and could really make the difference for someone else when they're wondering whether or not to take a chance on me and my writing. If you enjoyed the book and tell them why, it's possible your words will make them click the buy button, too! Just hop on over to wherever you bought this book – Amazon, Apple Books, Kobo, Bella Books, Barnes & Noble or any of the other digital outlets – and say what's in your heart. I always appreciate honest reviews.

Thank you, you're the best.

Love,
Clare x

Also by Clare Lydon

The All I Want Series

All I Want For Christmas (Book 1)

All I Want For Valentine's (Book 2)

All I Want For Spring (Book 3)

All I Want For Summer (Book 4)

All I Want For Autumn (Book 5)

Other Novels

A Taste Of Love

Before You Say I Do

Nothing To Lose: A Lesbian Romance

Once Upon A Princess

The Long Weekend

Twice In A Lifetime

You're My Kind

The London Romance Series

London Calling (Book 1)

This London Love (Book 2)

A Girl Called London (Book 3)

The London Of Us (Book 4)

London, Actually (Book 5)

Made In London (Book 6)

Printed in Great Britain
by Amazon